Firecrackers

Firecrackers

A Realistic Novel

Carl Van Vechten

MINT EDITIONS

Firecrackers: A Realistic Novel was first published in 1925.

This edition published by Mint Editions 2021.

ISBN 978-1-5131-3286-0

Published by Mint Editions®

minteditionbooks.com

Publishing Director: Jennifer Newens
Design & Production: Rachel Lopez Metzger
Project Manager: Micaela Clark
Typesetting: Westchester Publishing Services

"Et puis, pour nous les rendre supportables et sans remords, ne faut-il pas anoblir un peu toutes nos distractions?"

—Octave Mirbeau

"'There's no sort of use in knocking,' said the Footman, 'and that for two reasons. First, because I'm on the same side of the door as you are: secondly, because they're making such a noise inside, no one could possibly hear you.'"

—Lewis Carroll

"The worst of life is, nearly everybody marches to a different tune."

—The Archduchess: The Flower beneath the Foot

"Un peu trop c'est juste assex pour moi."

—Jean Cocteau

"I do not think we are so unhappy as we are vain, or so malicious as silly; so mischievous as trifling, or so miserable as we are vile."

—Michel de Montaigne

"We acquire the knowledge of that which we deserve to know."

—P. D. Ouspensky

Contents

One

Paul Moody permitted the book he had been attempting to read to slip from his relaxed finger-tips to the floor; his eyes wore that glazed, unseeing expression which is the outward token of vague thinking. It had been, indeed, impossible for him to invoke any interest in this novel, although, by a manifest effort, he had succeeded in turning the forty-third page. The fable, as he hazily recalled it in his chaotic reverie, dealt with a young American boy kept by a rich woman in her middle years. This relationship had been assumed some months before the episode occurred with which the story opened, a scene of sordid disillusion laid in a Paris restaurant. It had been on page forty-three that the boy began to explain to a sympathetic friend the trend of events which had led up to this situation. It was, Paul felt rather than thought, too much like life to be altogether agreeable, and he was certain that he could not entertain the idea of discovering, through the hardy means of a continued perusal, that the youth had made this compromise in order to secure release from a distasteful environment. Paul himself was sufficiently well acquainted with compromise to make the inspection of it, even in a literary aspect, uninviting.

There was, it became more and more evident to Paul, no escape from the rigorous luxury of his existence to be found in literature; certainly, life itself no longer offered an excuse for the gaping jaw of awe or astonishment. Even Campaspe Lorillard, he recalled with a little pang, appeared to have settled down; at any rate she was tired of inventing means for making the days and nights pleasant and capriciously variable for others. She had, it might be, determined to look out for herself in these respects and empower her friends to do likewise, were they fortunate enough to possess the necessary imaginative resources. Well, he was not fortunate enough, that was quite clear. Polish his wits as he would, he could summon up no vision of a single thing that he wanted to do. Was there, he demanded hopelessly of the great god Vacuum, anything to do? Paul assured himself that he was feeling very piano.

Slouching indolently, he sauntered to the window, where he watched the great sweeps of winter rain swirl against the protecting pane. Outside it was brumous: desolate and lonely; no one seemed to be passing by. Abruptly, from a crossing thoroughfare, a great truck lurched into the street and rolled, rumbling, towards Paul's vision. In the circle of light created by an overhead arc-lamp Paul descried the young driver in his leathern apron, his head bare, his thick, black hair matted by the drenching downpour, controlling the sturdy carthorses, the reins bound round his naked, brawny arms. In the eyes of this young carter, seen but an instant in passing, Paul fancied he recognized a gleam of enthusiasm, a stubborn relish, a defiance of the storm, which had once been his own. Had I been content to drive a truck, Paul considered, I, too, might have retained some of the sensation of the joy of living.

As he turned away from the window it occurred to him that some one else might have harboured this thought at one time or another, but a pendent, solacing reflection informed him that all overmastering emotions, of whatever nature, must have come down through the ages. That, he mused, is the whole secret of the trouble with us damned, restless spirits, there are no new overmastering emotions. What I am feeling now I have felt before, only never before so poignantly. There is nothing new to think, or to feel, or to do. Even unhappiness has become a routine tremor.

At this juncture Paul lighted a cigarette and struck, not wholly unself-consciously, an attitude of supreme dejection, head hanging from shoulders at an angle of forty-five degrees, before the augite fireplace which was the decorative centre of interest in the room. His lowered glance focused on the hearth and he was somewhat astonished to observe, and was at once aware of a slight lift in his melancholy as a result—so little external pressure is required to sway a mood—that no fire had been laid. He was also cognizant for the first time, although he had been occupying the room for half-an-hour, that he felt chilled. Lifting the pleated taffeta hanging from the seat under the windows, he stroked the pipes of the radiator. He touched cold metal, metal algid as ice! What could these passive signs portend? He could not recollect that this particular phenomenon had ever previously attracted his attention. His spirits rose as he pressed a button set in the wall.

He questioned the parlour-maid.

Mrs. Moody said that a fire in the drawing-room would be enough. I did not know that you had come in, sir.

But I never sit in the drawing-room before dinner.

She did not seek an alternative, explanatory phrase. I did not know that you had come in, sir, she repeated.

Well, light one now.

Very good, sir.

Choosing a journal from the loose heap of periodicals on the table, once more he settled himself in a renewed effort to read. To his disgust he discovered that he had selected a literary review. He examined the pile again, this time more carefully, but with no better success. It appeared that *all* the magazines were literary reviews—presumably Vera had raked out the fiction weeklies and carried them off to her own room—but a name on the cover of one of these arrested his attention. It was the name of the author of the novel, Two on the Seine, which he had so lately discarded. He flipped the pages until he found a paper about the fellow, together with his portrait.

Cynical chap, like me, was Paul's mental comment, only harder, much harder. There's bitterness there. He sighed. It's what we all come to, I suspect. Nothing to do. Well, he writes novels; at least he has that much the better of me. And, of course, he's older. I suppose I'll look even worse at his age. Paul compared his memory of the truckman, valiant, buoyant, steaming with wet, and yet apparently excited and happy, with the face on the open page before him, but he was not able to arrive at any conclusion.

The parlour-maid had returned with the logs sheltered neatly in the curve of her arm. My God, why was everything so damned neat? Nothing dislocated, nothing tortured, just everlasting neatness! As symmetrical, his world, he surmised, as the two halves of a circle before Einstein.

I forgot to ask you, Jennie—he addressed the figure kneeling in front of the fireplace—what's the matter with the furnace?

She turned her pretty, smiling face in his direction—even she, he noted, was like a rubber-stamp, like a maid in a French farce or a girl on the cover of a magazine—as she replied, The furnace is out of order, sir. I thought you knew.

Out of order! His spirits were soaring. If his luck continued he might be able to reconstruct a semblance of his quondam self. On second thought he recalled that Vera had announced this inconvenience earlier in the day. Now, however, it was evening.

But that was this morning, he objected aloud.

I know, sir. Jennie was engaged in expertly laying the fire. The man is still down there. He's acting very strange, sir.

Strange! How strange?

Well, while she was eating lunch, Mrs. Moody asked me to go see how he was getting along, and I did. He was reading a book, sir!

Reading a book!

Yes, sir. I came back and told Mrs. Moody and she thought it might be a recipe-book for fixing furnaces.

Good God! Paul tossed the magazine in his hand across the room. Have you been down since?

Twice, sir. Jennie applied the match.

Was he still reading?

The girl rose and brushed out her apron.

No, sir, she replied. The first time, he spoke to me, sir.

What did he say?

I don't know, sir. Something in a foreign language, sir.

Something in a foreign language. And the second time?

He was standing on his head, sir.

I think, Paul remarked, that I shall be obliged to go down and look this fellow over for myself.

Traversing the long corridor which led to the rear of the house, he crossed the kitchen and descended the cellar-steps, pressing a button to brighten his way. Passing through the laundry, walled with Nile-green tiles, he opened the door leading to the furnace-room. Pausing for an instant on the threshold of this vast, vaulted basement, the ceiling of which was upheld by a forest of terra-cotta columns, he experienced the distinct impression that he was listening to far-away music. A line of pillars, casting great shadows across the path ahead of him, completely blocked his view of the furnace. After a little, he pressed forward, instinctively walking softly on his toes, until, as the ranks of columns fell behind him, in the circular clearing in the centre of which rose the furnace, he was confronted with an amazing spectacle. On the stone-flagged pavement a youth reclined on his belly, his chin sustained by his palms, his forearms supported by his elbows. The young man, who might have been twenty-two years old, was absorbed in the pages of a book spread flat before him.

Paul, utterly unbeheld as yet, rested immobile for a moment while he studied the picture. The attitude of the young man, and his appearance, save for the fact that he wore the overalls of his craft, would have fitted into a fantastic sylvan ballet. His hair was black and sleek, like the coat of a seal just emerged from the ocean, his figure, slender, lithe, and taut, giving at once the impression of a distinguished grace and a superior strength. His hands were white and fragile, with long, delicate fingers. For the time being Paul was unable to see his face.

At last, but even so a little hesitantly, Paul moved forward and spoke.

Are you the chap who is supposed to be putting the furnace in order? he demanded.

Turning a leaf, rather than his head, the youth responded, I am.

Paul adopted a more aggressive tone. Then, why the devil don't you do it? The house is freezing.

This rougher method of approach was successful in disturbing the workman's preoccupation. He lowered his right forearm and permitted his neck to pivot until his gaze met the eyes of the intruder.

Who are you? he questioned softly. The rich resonance of his voice, the complete poise of his manner, the refined beauty of his face, cut as cleanly as a Roman sculptor might have carved it from marble, and as white as marble, his eyes, lustrous and black, his magenta lips, all were sufficiently baffling in the circumstances.

Moody is my name, Paul replied. I had supposed you were engaged to put the furnace in order. I. . .

The young man was on his feet at once and there was an implication of the miraculous even in the accomplishment of this movement which offered evidence of that co-ordinating control of the muscles which is the basis for all great dancing. Still, there was an expression of regret on the youth's countenance, adumbrating that he had been awakened from some bright dream. Again Paul thought he caught the distant tinkle of ancient music.

I beg your pardon, the youth apologized. The furnace has been in running order for some hours. I forgot—he was, in his embarrassment, almost stammering now—to notify the servants, but I will do so at once.

The boy spoke, Paul noted, with a slightly foreign, though unidentifiable, inflection, but not with an accent.

You won't mind my saying, Paul, now completely disarmed, put forward, that you are a most extraordinary fellow. Would you, he continued, mind telling me what you are reading?

The youth lovingly fingered the book which he still clasped in one hand. The Alchemy of Happiness, by the Persian poet-philosopher, Al-Ghazzali, was his response.

Good God! What is it about?

Al-Ghazzali avers that the highest function of man's soul is the perception of truth.

Paul rested a moment, silent, not without awe. When he spoke, it was to ask, Will you come upstairs? I'd like to talk with you.

By way of reply the youth mock-ruefully surveyed his stained overalls which contrasted violently with his well-kept hands, the delicate carving of his features.

Your clothes are all right. I don't want to talk with your clothes.

Then I'm with you.

The young man collected his scattered tools and packed them in a black hand-bag. The cherished volume by the Persian poet-philosopher he laid reverently on top. Now Paul led the way, the youth following, bag in hand, walking proudly, head erect, through the forest of terra-cotta columns and the green-tiled laundry, up the cellar steps, on across the kitchen, past the scandalized cook and maids, down the long corridor, back into the little chamber he had quitted but a few moments before. How different everything seemed now! The fire blazed fiercely, but it was not the fire which made the difference.

Sit down, Paul invited.

If you will permit me, I should like to wash my hands.

I beg your pardon. Paul made the carrying out of this reasonable request possible. Then he attended the youth's return.

Presently the workman came back into the room and accepted Paul's interrupted invitation. The rain continued to beat against the resounding panes, the fire crackled, but for a time neither of the men spoke. It became evident to Paul, at last, that a person with so much poise would never speak unless he had something to say and some good reason for saying it.

Will you have a little drink? Paul suggested.

Thank you, I don't drink, the young man replied, his gaze directed towards the cheer of the fire.

Smoke? Paul offered him the contents of a crystal box.

Not that either. The young man smiled.

Suddenly Paul broke out: See here. . . Then: How the devil does it happen that you're a furnace-man?

I'm not. At any rate, after tonight I'm not. I've done that. You appear to possess an excellent library.

It's not mine, at least most of it isn't. These—Paul swept his arm towards the full cases which lined the walls—are bindings, not books. I doubt if you'd find anything to read, *there.*

I'm not so sure.

What do you like to read?

Instead of replying to this question, the young man asseverated solemnly, What you lack is balance.

Balance?

Balance.

But. . .

Plumbing, the young man announced, and the allied artisanships serve their purposes. He rose, and with the utmost nonchalance stooped to toss a log on the waning blaze in the fireplace. Max Beerbohm's dictum that you should never poke a friend's fire unless the friendship dates back at least seven years invaded Paul's mind, and yet he did not feel resentful.

For a few moments the only sounds audible in the chamber were the crackling of the fire and the wailing of the wind smiting the chimney. Then the young man spoke again.

Have you ever thought of the meaning of life? he inquired.

I don't ever think of anything else! I've been thinking about it all the afternoon.

Well, what conclusion did you reach? Does it lie in service? or delight? or the approach to nonexistence?

I had about decided to give up the search. . . I had come to the conclusion that it had no meaning. . . until. . . What is it? What does it mean?

You see I'm not a preacher, the young man appeared to be apologizing.

Not a preacher!

I have had, perhaps, a vision, a glimpse of something, but why try to explain it?

But if I'm interested.

Paul actually quivered as the word passed his lips.

I'll tell you what, he went on, and then, interrupting himself with a Wait a minute, he rang the bell.

Jennie, he demanded when the maid appeared, what's Mrs. Moody doing?

She's dining out, sir.

O, yes, I remember. . . Mr. eh. . . Benson is dining with me. You might serve dinner in this room.

Yes, sir. Jennie looked as if she were about to give notice.

And wait a minute. Tell Albert to build a fire in the furnace.

Yes, sir.

There!

I'm sure it will be most pleasant, the youth avowed. You should have good food. Persons without balance. . .

O, hell! What's the formula, the password, the keynote? What is it, this balance?

It's a pity, the stranger remarked abruptly, that Hell's Kitchen, Battle Row, and Corcoran's Roost have been cleaned up. They were gone before I arrived in America. I long for a battle with the Hudson Duster Gang. I burn for an encounter with Mike the Mauler and the Bad Wop. I crave an introduction to Big Jack Zelig, Kid Twist, and Louie the Lump. I regret the obsequies of Kid Dropper. Where are Tanner Smith, Big Jim Redmond and Rubber Shaw? Where is the Gas House Gang?

Damned if I know! Would you really like to meet them?

Would I! Not in this rain, not in the taxi that will carry me away from here, but some time, some night, I'd like to, and now they're gone.

Paul scrutinized the countenance of the youth whose brow seemed knitted with despair. He was losing patience.

See here, he exclaimed. Give it to me. . . what you've got. It's what I need. It's what I hoped there would be! This complete and fascinating dislocation!

Jennie was pulling out the supports of a gate-legged table.

It isn't mine any more than it's yours. I can't *give it* to you.

Explain! Explain!

I'm not a preacher, the youth said for the second time.

Who are you?

I'm the boiler-mender you met in the cellar and invited to dine with you.

Can you really stand on your head?

Do you doubt it?

Will you?

You will.

I think I'm standing on my head at this moment.

From the time the soup appeared, on through the salad, the young man ate ravenously. Until he explained that he had forgotten to eat any lunch, Paul fancied that he must have been hungry for days. And while the youth devoured his food he largely refrained from speech. Paul, whose stomach suffered no pangs, regarded the fellow with esurient eyes, the eyes of an avid curiosity. What was it the chap had, and why wouldn't he tell?

Did you, the stranger queried at last, ever hear of Hippias?

Never, Paul replied, and then eagerly demanded, Tell me about him.

Or Leonardo?

Of course, I've heard of him. You mean The Last Supper guy.

Yes. The young man stared at Paul, and his stare at even a low rate of intensity had almost the devastating force of a gimlet. I think, he went on, that I'd like to tell you about Darwin's profligate bees.

Profligate bees?

Yes. It seems that some colonial or other carried a hive of thrifty English bees over to the West Indies. After the first year they ceased to save up their honey, as they found no occasion to use it. The weather was so splendid, the flowers so plentiful, that the bees sloughed off their serious businesslike habits, became profligate and debauched, devoured their capital, determined to labour no longer, and entertained themselves by flying about the islands and stinging the Negroes.

Jennie chose this inopportune moment to announce that Mrs. Moody was calling on the telephone.

What the devil! Paul exclaimed, and then, Excuse me, just a moment. When, after a longer absence than he had foretold—Vera had kept him for an interminable period—he returned, he found the room empty. Instinct informed him that something else had disappeared along with the fantastic boiler-mender and presently, running his eye over the late Mr. Whittaker's bookshelves, he discovered a gap in the otherwise uninterrupted phalanx of volumes.

Two

Consuelo is causing me a great deal of anxiety.

Having delivered herself of this baleful bit of information, Laura Everest bent forward to manipulate her Sheffield tea-service. She poured out a cup for Campaspe Lorillard and, without asking her preferences in flavouring, dropped in two rose cubes of sugar, together with a little cream.

One lump and lemon, please, Campaspe protested, rejecting the proffered cup.

O dear, I forgot. I can't get Consuelo off my mind.

While Laura was arranging the exchange, Campaspe's eyes roved round the drawing-room, apparently appraising the Jacobean lacquer, the Chippendale chairs, and the portrait by Sir William Orpen of Laura Everest in the gown in which she had been presented at Buckingham, although years before she would have been able to make an inventory of every object in the room for an insurance inspector, so thoroughly was she acquainted with each one of them.

Ostensibly reflective, she stirred the contents of her cup. Yes, dear? she put forward at last, seemingly with no tinge of curiosity—it appeared as if she had noted that Laura was determined to talk and was not unwilling to permit her to exercise this desire—You were speaking of Consuelo.

I just can't think what the world's coming to, Laura continued. When we were young girls I don't think we ever raised problems for our parents.

Don't be ridiculous, Laura. You're only thirty-six yourself at this minute.

You know very well what I mean, Campaspe. Consuelo is ten.

The only sign of impatience Campaspe betrayed was a nervous tapping of her foot on the rug.

She's too young to be really young, she remarked cryptically.

That's just it, Campaspe: she's ages older than I am. Were we like that?

Like what, Laura?

Laura gave no indication that she had heard this query. She lifted a spray of freesia from a green glass vase on the tea-table and held it to her nostrils as she murmured, It's just too awful!

What has she done?

It isn't that she's done anything, at least not yet, at least not much of anything. It is, Laura wailed, the things she thinks, the things she says.

You might let her talk with Basil. He hasn't a single idea in his head that couldn't be found in a novel by Frances Hodgson Burnett. I think I'll have a langue de chat.

Now Campaspe, Laura pleaded, passing the plate, don't tease me. I'm really quite serious.

I'm not teasing you, Laura.

You are too absurd, Campaspe. Besides, I don't think she'd want to listen to Basil. He's much too young for her. She prefers men of forty, men of the world. She was completely fascinated by Paul Moody the other day. I really don't like to have him come here any more.

What *are* her ideas?

It's not one thing. It's just everything she says and thinks. Indeed, I'm certain she thinks even worse things than she says. You know how careful I've always been. I've engaged the *best* governesses, the *very* best. Miss Pinchon is particularly to be relied upon. Eugenia, Laura concluded sadly, isn't a bit like Consuelo.

For the moment Campaspe gave up any idea of proceeding further along this direct line; she opened, rather, an oblique attack. Speaking of Paul, she began, I'm worried about *him.* I've never really worried about him before because he has always managed somehow to light on his feet, no matter how many storeys high the window from which he was tossed, but Vera seems too much for him.

I never considered that marriage proper, Laura announced severely. She's much older than he is—over twice his age, I should think—and it's perfectly obvious that he married her for her money. I knew it would turn out badly. It was *certain* to.

It hasn't turned out so badly in one way, Campaspe averred reflectively, as she began to count the coins in a Russian leather purse she had extracted from her hand-bag. He's been well taken care of. The late Mr. Whittaker's house is quite handsome in its sombre fashion, and Paul understands the art of arranging a dinner. Even Vera knows how to do that. But he's getting seedy, rusty. . . brain-fag, or the kind of fag that Paul would have instead of brain-fag. Why, I asked him to supper the other night, a very dull supper for some stupid professors, and he actually came. It discouraged me. The next thing we know Paul will go gaga.

It's his conscience, Laura asseverated sternly, getting the better of him. He knows that he has done wrong and he can get no more pleasure out of life. No one, she asserted categorically, can marry a fat, middle-aged woman for her money and remain happy.

You may be right, Laura. Campaspe yawned. What time is it getting to be?

Laura consulted her wrist. Around six. My watch is slow or fast, I forget which. Do you really want to know?

Approximately. I've got to. . .

Mrs. Moody, the maid announced.

Dear Vera, Laura rose to greet her caller.

Dear Laura, and Campaspe!

Vera, what a pleasure!

The stout woman, swathed in broadtail, waddled in, and settled herself in a deep arm-chair. I've just come from the matinee. She spoke in a squeaky, ineffectual voice, which seemed oddly at variance with her vast exterior. The odour of Tabac Blond pervaded the atmosphere.

Laura handed her a cup of tea, into which she had dropped one lump of sugar and a slice of lemon.

Fata Morgana. . . Laura, you *know* I take cream and *two* lumps.

O, I'm sorry. Of course, you do. Was it a good play?

Horrible. Not in the least like life. A middle-aged woman makes love to a boy. I detest sex abnormalities. A ridiculous situation, I think.

Absurd! Campaspe commented.

Laura was silent.

And do you know, Gareth Johns's new novel is based on the same disgusting subject? . . . Vera inspected the tray of sweets. . . I think I'll have two of these amandines de Provence. Are they fattening? I don't want to get fat. . . A perfectly idiotic affair between a boy and a middle-aged woman living together in Paris. Stupid! What are we coming to?

Stupid, perhaps, Campaspe remarked, but not entirely untrue to life. It's his own story, or part of it.

You know him!

The Countess Nattatorrini, whom he deserted years ago, is a friend of mine. O, it all happened in the late nineties. She's seventy-seven now.

Seventy-seven! gasped Vera, almost choking over her tea. How revolting!

She wasn't seventy-seven when she lived with Gareth, you must remember.

How old was she then? Laura was able to get out. It was impossible for her to become reconciled to the fact that Vera Moody, who weighed two-hundred and fifty pounds and had certainly passed her fifty-fifth birthday, had chosen this subject for conversation.

About fifty, I think, Campaspe replied, staring directly at Vera.

Well, all the more, if it *did* happen, he ought to keep still about it, was Vera's decision. It's very unusual, *very.*

She lifted an amandine in her chubby fingers to her lips. There was almost an air of cannibalism about Vera eating, Campaspe thought.

I saw Florizel Hammond at the theatre, Mrs. Moody went on. He was telling me about Frederic Richards. It seems that he charges twice as much to paint a brunette as he does to paint a blonde, brunettes are so distasteful to him.

What's Paulet doing? Campaspe yawned again. She was beginning to wonder whether her hour had been wasted.

As her husband's name was pronounced, Vera sat up very straight, carefully placed her cup of tea on a nearby pear-wood table, and gave every evidence in the expressive working of her features of the liveliest excitement. Paul, she announced—she was shriller even than usual—had the most extraordinary experience yesterday with a boiler-mender.

Did he beat Paulet up? Campaspe demanded.

No. It was stranger than that. He asked the man to dine with him.

Alert at last, Campaspe inquired, Did the fellow accept the invitation?

Yes, he did, and they had a curious conversation, but Paul can't remember a word of it, and then the man disappeared. Paul blames me for that. . . Vera was almost crying now. Her words were pronounced in a whimper. . . He complains that I telephoned at the wrong moment and interrupted them, but how could I know, Campaspe, that Paul was dining with a boiler-mender? I'm sure he has no right to blame me. I. . .

Where did he meet him? Campaspe broke in.

In the basement. He was fixing the furnace. He *had* fixed it, as a matter of fact. Paul found him reading the Persian poets. . .

The Persian poets! Campaspe echoed.

In the basement! What is the world coming to? Laura shook her head deprecatingly.

and standing on his head, Vera completed her sentence, goggling about her wildly. What *do* you make of it?

The sound of a child's voice in the hall interrupted the possibility of making anything of it for the present.

O, Consuelo has returned from the matinee! Laura cried. Her Aunt Jessie offered to take her. It is so difficult to select a suitable play for a child to see nowadays that I just told Jessie to take her to whatever the Theatre Guild was doing. They always present nice, clean plays, I've heard.

Why, Laura, she's only ten! Vera exclaimed.

Campaspe laughed outright.

What *is* the matter, Vera? Laura demanded. What *are* they playing at the Garrick?

Campaspe supplied the necessary information: Fata Morgana.

For her entrance Consuelo chose the moment that Laura had selected to exhibit her anguish. Opening the ivory-enamelled folding doors, the child paused for an instant on the threshold, long enough for her mother's callers to take in the exquisite picture. Long, curly, golden hair framed a pale and wistful face in which elusive, pansy-blue eyes were the most prominent feature. Consuelo was wrapped in a cloak of sable which did not quite reach her socks, permitting an inch or two of slender, bare leg to show. On her head she wore a sable toque and she carried a cluster of green orchids.

Maman, the child inquired, do I intrude?

Not at all, dear. Come in. You know Mrs. Lorillard and Mrs. Moody.

Indeed, yes, the child responded gravely. How do you do? And how is Mr. Moody? We had such a long talk the other afternoon.

Mr. Moody is quite well, thank you, my dear, Vera replied, in the gushing tone she always adopted when addressing children and kittens.

Consuelo turned away from her and seated herself very precisely in a great Louis XVI needle-point arm-chair. It is very warm here, she remarked.

Why don't you take off your cloak, Consuelo? Laura suggested. Where did you get those orchids?

The child did not remove her cloak. Aunt Jessie bought them for me, she replied. At least she asked me what I wanted her to buy for me, and I selected orchids. I *do not* care for candy, do you, Mrs. Lorillard?

Not particularly, was that lady's response. I'm sure I prefer orchids.

So do I, Consuelo averred placidly; they're so expensive, expensive and aristocratic. I adore the aristocratic gesture. I read somewhere recently that Ludwig, the mad King of Bavaria, would not permit a dentist to contaminate his palace. When he was forced to have a tooth extracted, the dentist stood in the royal garden and the monarch stuck his head out of the window. . . Maman, you might give me a cup of tea. *Three* lumps, you know, and no cream or lemon.

Laura's hand trembled as she lifted the pot.

So *you* tell her? Campaspe smiled.

Don't *you,* Mrs. Lorillard? You know maman never remembers anything, that is anything like *that,* do you, maman? I tell papa that she does not retain.

Mrs. Everest was too much upset for her lips to form words. She handed her harassing daughter her cup of tea, flavoured according to specifications, and Consuelo, after taking a sip, and emitting an involuntary, Um, it's good! turned again to Mrs. Lorillard, completely shutting out Mrs. Moody, who sat on the other side of the child.

Do tell me, please, she urged, a good book to read. I run through everything so quickly.

What have you been reading lately? Campaspe demanded.

O, everything in papa's library and maman's library, and the books Aunt Jessie gives me, and a few others besides, that I pick up here and there. You know papa never reads—Aunt Jessie once told me that he started The Old Wives' Tale the day after he and maman were married, and I'm sure he hasn't finished it yet—but he buys lots of books because he likes to have his library filled up, and so I climb about in there until I dig out something amusing.

Consuelo, you know mama has told you not to read too much. Laura flushed. Fortunately, for the child's taste, she explained, her father buys only the *best* books.

Consuelo did not appear to be particularly aware of this inconsiderate interruption. You were asking me, Mrs. Lorillard, she remarked, what I had been reading. It would take me an hour to make out the catalogue. I'd better limit myself to telling you what I like best of the books I have read recently.

Do, Campaspe urged.

Well, first, I think, the Memoirs of William Hickey, and after that, Antic Hay. . .

Laura settled back in her chair more comfortably. I *am* relieved, she said, to learn that you are reading memoirs, Consuelo dear. They are always so solid. Don't you think it wonderful, Campaspe, Consuelo reading memoirs at her age? Now, you and I. . .

I do, indeed, Campaspe responded. Then, turning again to the child, What do you think of the period, Consuelo?

Well, Hickey was all right and I liked the *parties,* and it was enjoyable and old-fashioned and *homey.* I think life has changed a great deal since the eighteenth century. We seem to drink more now, at least in America. And do you believe, Mrs. Lorillard, that a play like Fata Morgana would have been possible then? A splendid, cynical play, with a touch of romance under it. Why, it's almost sentimental in spots! It was so sweet and naïve of that boy to carry on so about that lovely lady, and you know perfectly well when she leaves him crying over his books to return to Buda-Pesth with her husband that he will join her before the month is up. As for me, I couldn't bear to see them separated even for a moment.

And what did daughter do after the play? Laura demanded, in an effort to create some kind of diversion.

O, I forgot! Consuelo continued consistently to address Campaspe. I had such a beautiful experience. It happened at the florist's. A perfect darling of a young man waited on me. He was as handsome as. . . as. . . as a Peri. When I told him I wanted orchids he pronounced them just the flowers for me, and he quoted one of the Persian poets. . .

The Persian poets! Vera exclaimed.

Yes, a philosopher-poet named Al-Ghazzali, and that started us going and I think I should have been there yet, but Aunt Jessie was *so* impatient. She really dragged me away. He was such a nice young man, and so handsome and so intelligent and he had such a curious philosophy of life.

What was his philosophy of life? Campaspe demanded eagerly.

The child's expression was vague. I had to *sense* that, she explained. He didn't, you see, *exactly* tell me. I'd rather talk to you about it some day when we're alone. Maman wouldn't understand, and it would bore her.

A sudden memory transfused the wistfulness in the child's white face with a radiant variety of delight. Her nostrils twitched like the fins of a goldfish as she groped about in her hand-bag. He gave me his card, she explained. She brought it forth triumphantly at last and handed it to Campaspe. That lady, no longer in doubt about the value of the manner in which she had been passing her time, read thereon:

GUNNAR O'GRADY

Acrobat

Three

The following foreday Campaspe found it imperative to employ the telephone twice. First, she called up Paulet to ask him to bring his boiler-mender to luncheon. He was, it was simple to deduce from the timbre of his voice, in a highly shattered mood, as nervous as a race-horse pawing the turf before the tape. Nothing, he assured her, would give him more pleasure than the ability to satisfy her desire, but he happened to be ignorant of the address of his esoteric guest. Should he come alone? The reply to this proposal was a decorous but curt No. Having thus summarily concluded this extremely unsatisfactory interview, Campaspe demanded another number from the recalcitrant operator. Laura Everest was the second person Mrs. Lorillard honoured with her early morning voice. She inquired if Consuelo might lunch with her at the Ritz—Basil, home from school convalescing after a slight illness, was coming too. However much this request may have disturbed Laura, she assented to the plan, and so a little before one the Lorillard motor stopped in front of the East Sixty-eighth Street house, where the Everests made their home, to pick up Consuelo.

Once the child was settled beside her in the car, Campaspe offered to buy her orchids. Couldn't we, she suggested, find the florist who sold you those magnificent flowers yesterday? Consuelo clapped her hands. I'll see Mr. O'Grady again, was her happy rejoinder. Campaspe hoped and believed she would, but when she spoke again it was merely to demand directions for finding the place. There occurred, just here, a hitch in the arrangements. Consuelo, it appeared, was uncertain as to the exact locality. She recalled that Aunt Jessie's car had turned from Thirty-sixth Street into Fifth Avenue, and that they had driven north for several blocks, but somewhere or other a caprice of the chauffeur had occasioned them to make a slight detour, so that a few hundred yards on Madison Avenue, together with two side streets, had been included in the route. The possibility that the flowers had been purchased on one of these increased the child's perplexity. Campaspe, who experienced a fierce desire to shake her, contented herself with urging gently, Try to recall the neighbourhood, dear. Doesn't a sign or the appearance of an adjacent shop come into your mind? Consuelo, who had her own compelling reasons for making this tour of rediscovery successful, was obliged to admit that her mind was apparently a complete blank in regard to these matters. Before they had entered the florist's door she had been in a listless mood and had given no heed to her surroundings, and after they had come out her state of excitement had equally prevented her from paying attention to marks of identification for which she could summon up no immediate interest. The child wracked her brains for a potential clue. It would have proved amusing, had Campaspe's impatience given her leave to enjoy such an emotion, to observe the miniature knit of the parthenic brow, to watch the little girl bury her frail face fecklessly in her hands with their tapering fingers. Basil, as usual, was silent. In any case he could be of no assistance. While these desperate sacrifices were being offered on the altar of Mnemosyne, the automobile rested dormant before the door of the Sixty-eighth Street house.

I know! Consuelo cried at last, as the light of a new intelligence shone in her eyes. There were stuffed doves in the window.

It seemed a remote beacon, but as it was unique, Campaspe ordered Ambrose to follow the trail. Now, while the chauffeur drove the car forward, every nose was snubbed against a pane, every eye sought for the vision of a stuffed dove. Consuelo was vague in regard to the number of blocks to be traversed on Madison Avenue, but she issued general directions which proved to be the reverse of helpful. When, after they had been held up at nearly every crossing by a policeman regulating traffic, they attained Thirty-sixth Street without having encountered a single stuffed dove, the quest appeared to be vain. Campaspe, however, was not to be so easily discouraged. Were it necessary she was quite prepared to engage a secretary merely for the purpose of calling up every florist listed in the classified telephone directory to inquire which of them kept stuffed doves. It was still possible to demand first aid of Jessie Hardy or her chauffeur, but, for the moment, while Ambrose drew up the car in front of Page and Shaw's, Campaspe contented herself by appealing to Consuelo to pray ardently once more to the mother of the Muses. Quite suddenly and unexpectedly, the prayer was answered. There had been, Consuelo was at last aware, a silversmith next door, in whose show-window silver pheasants and chased metal kings with ivory faces were displayed. To Campaspe, who was as well acquainted with this part of New York as she was with her own mind, this was an adequate signal. She gave Ambrose the requisite commands and soon the motor paused before the proper portal. The doves—inquiry elicited this information—had been removed only that morning in favour of fresher decorations. O'Grady, too, had taken his departure. Orchids, however, were obviously still in stock.

Very odd, Mrs. Lorillard, the shop-keeper was explaining, a very odd case. O'Grady was here yesterday and he is gone today. The best salesman I ever had. Willingly, I would have offered him twice the money to stay with me.

Had he been with you long? the furious Campaspe demanded.

Only since yesterday morning. I had advertised for a salesman and he walked in about eight o'clock, along with ten other fellows. I engaged O'Grady; he worked all day; and last night he walked out. Nothing is missing; he did not even ask for his wages. He simply walked out and hasn't come back. I can't understand it!

Consuelo's disappointment was as keen as Campaspe's, but, after all, there was the matter of her orchids. She broached the subject.

The florist opened the glass doors of his brilliantly illuminated refrigerator.

Didn't you take down his address? Campaspe persisted.

No. I can't think why. It's the first time such a thing has ever happened. We *always* take down our employees' addresses. Stupid girl! He shook his fist at the cashier. That self-sufficient blonde was busily engaged in reading a novel by J. S. Fletcher and her absorption spared her a knowledge of the insulting gesture.

He was a particularly *nice* young man, Consuelo asseverated with dignity. I think, Mrs. Lorillard, I prefer the green ones to the mauve ones.

Are the orchids for the little girl? the florist inquired. In that case let me unpack a few white sprays that have just come in.

Pray, don't trouble, Consuelo remarked, a trifle scornfully. I prefer the green ones.

As the troop evacuated, Basil spoke at last.

Mama, he begged, may I have chocolate ice-cream at the Ritz?

PAUL, IN THE MEANTIME, DEPRIVED of Campaspe's company at luncheon, ate a silent meal across the table from Vera. Several times she attempted to tell him about Consuelo's adventure in the flower-shop, but he was too preoccupied to listen. As soon as possible he returned to what had been his employment a good part of the morning, pacing up and down his little library, or at any rate the room which was *his* little library now. This chamber had originally been the pride of Bristol

Whittaker, who had enjoyed a fancy for fine bindings and had indulged this taste extensively in orders and purchases from René Kieffer, Léon Gruel, Cobden Sanderson, Marius Michel, Noulhac, Canape, Mercier, Lortic, and the dealers in the work of dead binders. So long as the toolings were elaborate Whittaker had cared nothing about the contents of his collection and the volumes were indifferently by Ernest Renan, Pierre Loti, Gyp, Eliphas Lévi, Wilkie Collins, Mark Twain, and Henry James. It was doubtful if Paul would ever read these books. Even his own books, scattered over the great Sheraton desk, were largely neglected.

On this particular day Paul was not thinking about books at all. He chose to be in this room merely because it was more sympathetic to him than any other chamber in the house. For the first time in his life, he really believed, he was experiencing an emotion quite foreign to his temperament, the emotion of unsatisfied curiosity. There was, after all, he had discovered quite unwittingly, something more in life after you had become convinced that there was nothing, another turn around a strange corner, another contingency of interest, but the apparition which had imparted this important knowledge to him had disappeared before he had been given a fair opportunity to discover wherein its special properties lay. The fellow had decamped with a couple of books, too, but Paul was not fretting over this loss. I'd give him the books, he muttered, just to have him here again.

On the whole, it seemed improbable to Paul that he would be able to gratify this desire. An interview with the furnace company which had supplied the young man had yielded barren results. O'Grady—that, apparently, was the fellow's inappropriate cognomen—had, beyond doubt, worked for the firm for ten days, giving, it appeared, almost a nimiety of satisfaction. He was, the boss informed Paul in an astonishing flow of language which seemed to spurt from Roget, a gem of the first water, a treasure, one in a thousand, a find, a nonesuch, a prodigy, and the salt of the earth. There was, indeed, no question but that he might successfully have demanded a substantial raise in wages. Instead, in the very middle of the week he had walked out, leaving no address behind him. Yes, it was customary for the firm to register the addresses of employees, but in this instance—the only case of the kind the boss could recall—some one had been careless. No, Mr. Moody could not possibly wish to find the fellow more than the furnace company did. The boss swore that he was almost ready to offer a reward for his apprehension. Possibly, O'Grady had met with foul play, even, perhaps, have been murdered, at least held in detention by some miscreant or other. There were, it was likely Mr. Moody had noted in the newspapers, kidnappers abroad. No hope of ransom in this case? The boss disillusioned Mr. Moody. He assured his questioner that he would be overjoyed to pay the ransom himself.

At least, from this interview, Paul had gleaned the suggestion of an advertisement. His first idea in regard to this public notice was worded in the following manner:

> If the young man who dined with Mr. Moody at 73 East Fifty-fifth Street on Wednesday evening will kindly communicate with Mr. Moody at that address he will learn something to his advantage.

This he ultimately discarded, formulating an alternative notice which was almost as odd as one he had once answered himself:

> Gunnar O'Grady: I don't want the books, but we did not finish our conversation. Will you come back?
>
> Paul Moody

He had caused this to be inserted in the New York World and the New York Times this very morning. In the meantime Paul's perplexity increased, and it would have afforded him infinite solace to lunch with Campaspe in order to discuss ways and means for unravelling this exceedingly tangled skein. Campaspe, however, apparently had been in no mood to receive anything less than exact information. She had definitely rejected his proposal. Palpably, he must go it alone.

Nevertheless, Paul was fully aware that pacing the floor, in the manner of an unhappy tiger in the zoo, would not help him to a solution of the mystery. He would end by suffering a splitting headache. As a matter of fact—and Paul was by no means ignorant of this idiosyncrasy—any attitude of mind save nonchalance was bad for him, morally, spiritually, and constitutionally. He determined, therefore, to make an effort to rid himself of this unpleasant mental condition. At least, while he paced, he might breathe fresh air. It was a warm day for the season of the year. The sun was shining and the pavements were dry. Paul drew on a light coat, grasped a Malacca stick, and ventured forth.

At first he strolled aimlessly this way and that, up and down the familiar thoroughfares near his home, glancing now and again apprehensively at some conspicuous window behind which might lurk a pair of spying eyes. Would any one observing him be conscious of the possibility that he was quite mad? he wondered. Turning, after a time, south on Park Avenue, he increased his speed, for, after all, he considered, as I am walking nowhere, the sooner I arrive the better. Then, noting a passing taxi which flaunted a green flag proclaiming the vehicle vacant, impulsively signalling the chauffeur to stop, he deposited himself within the car, curled himself up comfortably in the back seat, and lighted a cigarette.

Where to? the driver demanded.

Hell, I don't care. Flushing—confronted with the man's stare—he amended this to, I don't know, concluding a little lamely—inspired probably by the sight of two small boys engaged in fisticuffs on a nearby corner—The Battery.

The chauffeur drove his machine in the desired direction while Paul closed his eyes and smoked in a futile attempt to concentrate on a method for the solution of his irritating problem. His mind chose rather to consider the truth of a certain proverb: What one doesn't know does one no harm. How false! How utterly and completely false! Paul mused. Aside from having arrived at this important conclusion, his mind was as empty when he arrived at the Battery as it had been when he engaged the taxi. In spite of this disappointing state of affairs, following another impulse, he got out, paid the man, and entered the Aquarium.

At first, the tanks of fish, which he had never before inspected, served as a distraction. In turn he examined, not without interest, the white-fish swimming like pale ghosts, the mudfish, with their great sapphire eyes, only elsewhere to be discovered in nature on the wings of gaudy moths, set near the bases of their tails, the bony gar, resembling a dirigible, with its long tawny body, its extensive bony nose, and its under-fins, the great Jewfish, propelling itself fastuously about like a fish of a thousand years, the iridescent grouper, momentarily changing its colour, the green moray, so like a long, live, constantly waving velvet ribbon, the pretty sea-robins, the miraculous angel-fish, with their trusting, doglike eyes, fish that might have been created by Benozzo Gozzoli, and the parrot-fish, saffron and purple and turquoise-blue. It was amusing to watch these scaly creatures, so entirely self-satisfied, nosing around stupidly, displaying their vulgarly brilliant fins and turbine tails with complacency and pride, seeking flies and crumbs and discovering too often only bubbles, the bubbles that ascended incessantly behind the protecting vitrine from the depths of the tanks to the heights, like bright fountains of notes in the music of Ravel. All the paraphernalia here again, Paul thought, for another allegory about life and mankind. And the only man who knew the other secret, who was wise enough to understand how to be happy and intelligent at the same time, had vanished. It was some small comfort, anyway, to be aware that there existed one who *did* know, one who could explain if he so desired, even if it were impossible to find him.

Paul regarded, in passing, the sleek seal in the centre of the room; he cast a glance in the direction of the tortoises and the tiny salamanders, creatures conceived by God apparently for the sole purpose of inspiring the artisans who worked for François I. At last, somewhat harassed by the combined odours of fish and garlic, he left the Aquarium behind him, and cut straight across the Bowling Green. On he went, up Broadway, past Trinity Church, with its ancient tombstones mouldering in the peaceful churchyard, protected from the incongruous rush of public feet on the sidewalk by an iron grating, until he stood in a great square, where he paused to admire the Woolworth Building, a golden tower of fancy glittering in the afternoon sun, and the City Hall itself, as perfect an example of early American architecture, he remembered he had been informed some time or other, as could be seen in New York, and Paul realized that he had never seen it before. He had never before, indeed, save in an automobile, travelled south of Fourteenth Street.

His unpremeditated way now led him down Nassau Street and he noted the quaint names of the crossroads, Ann Street, John Street, Maiden Lane—he wondered if there might not be a Paul Place or a Campaspe Row. Cupid must work down here somewhere, was his pendent inspiration. That would be an idea, to call on Cupid. Determining to seek a drug-store where he might consult a telephone directory, he turned for this purpose into Ann Street. To Paul, this city by-way, with its Coca-Cola signs, pastry-shops, opticians, and billiard-parlours, seemed as strange as an odd corner of old London. A sign caught his attention: Dress Suits and Cutaways to Hire. In another window a clearance sale of ties, offered to prospective buyers for twenty-nine cents each, was announced. On the corner a group of Salvation Army lassies was singing At the Cross, and a silent vendor peddled the Birth-Control Review. The sidewalk was crowded with pedestrians scurrying in full festinance in both directions, but in front of one window, three loiterers had collected, two shingle-haired stenographers and a Postal Telegraph messenger boy. Automatically, unreasonably, Paul joined them.

Behind the glass, across which was blazoned in gold letters: Morris Shidrowitz—Suits, a young man was engaged in drawing on and off a coat, pointing at intervals during the ceremony to descriptive placards. Cheap, Classy, Comfortable, read one recommendation; another, Warm, Practical, Neat, Serviceable; while the third shrieked: See this detachable collar! The Warmknit Homespun Coat is the only coat made with a detachable collar. The actor in this utilitarian pantomime carried out his performance with the utmost gravity and efficiency. It was a pleasure to observe how one finger, poised at an identical angle with each repetition of the gesture, pointed to the succession of placards, how exactly similar was every like move the man made in every separate drawing on and off of the coat. Impelled, at last, to glance at the fellow's face, Paul very nearly shouted. It was he! The boiler-mender! Gunnar O'Grady, Esq. No other.

Paul tapped on the pane. Gunnar, who until thus signalled appeared to be entirely oblivious of the fact that he acted before an audience, looked straight out, his eyes meeting Paul's. Breaking the rhythm of his exhibition long enough to give a sign of recognition, even a greeting, in which there indubitably lurked an expression of delight, he held up five fingers. Immediately thereafter, he returned to the studied routine of his job.

The five fingers, Paul argued with himself, might indicate one of two ideas: five minutes or five o'clock. After, therefore, he had waited in front of the window for a quarter of an hour longer and had observed no variation in the manœuvres—O'Grady had not even looked his way again—Paul entered the shop. The girls, meanwhile, had taken their departure, but the messenger boy, fascinated, lingered.

A pimply-faced clerk, with hands like the flippers of the seal in the Aquarium, hurried to Paul's side.

Do you want a coat, mister? he demanded.

No. I want to interview that fellow in your window.

Eyeing the false customer with suspicion, the clerk made no move.

I'm not a detective, Paul averred defensively. Reflecting afterwards, it seemed to him that this had been an idiotic remark to make.

The clerk beckoned to the shop-keeper, an old and bearded Jew who wore a long, black coat and a skull cap.

I am interested, Paul explained, in the young man in your window.

No, we don't want to buy nothing, Mr. Shidrowitz rejoined.

He's deef, the clerk offered by way of enlightenment. You have to yell.

I want to talk with the man in the window! Paul shouted.

No, we don't want nobody in the window. The old man shook his head cautelously. We got him already this morning.

The clerk, waving his unseemly flippers, came to the rescue. You can't see him now. He's workin'.

What time does he get through?

Five o'clock.

Paul consulted his watch. It was now four. By way of making amends for his curious behaviour, he purchased two fiery red neckties, the first pair he picked up from a generous assortment, for fifty cents each. These, on his way out of the store, he promptly presented to the messenger boy, who accepted the gift, but not without grumbling that he wouldn't be caught drowneded in a red tie. Paul, after casting a long glance at the window for reassurance, started away. That last inspection had exposed to him Gunnar O'Grady in the act of underscoring the lines on the placard which descanted upon the superiority of the detachable collar of the Warmknit Homespun Coat. His ease and grace, his lack of self-consciousness, his facile assumption of this difficult and humiliating rôle, were matters for Paul's consideration during his next perturbed hour.

Four

At five o'clock—even a little before—Paul planted himself squarely in front of the shop of Morris Shidrowitz. It was dusk and all the windows along the street were illuminated. Crowds of young clerks, stenographers, and office-boys were pressing forward towards the gaping jaw of the subway. They jostled Paul uncomfortably and, in self-protection, he took up his position on the edge of the kerb. The exodus from the shop of Shidrowitz had begun. The pimply-faced clerk was the first to emerge, giving Paul a searching and somewhat impertinent stare before he was swept into the human stream, so like a river thickly peopled with a swimming school of salmon, soon to be netted and packed tightly in cans. The show-window, Paul observed, was unoccupied, but still O'Grady delayed. It was growing colder and the brisk wind which had blown up penetrated the light coat Paul was wearing. Once or twice, after the manner of a mummer impersonating a farmer in a down east melodrama, he extended his algid arms and then brought them together across his chest with a resounding thwack.

At last! His face lighted up with pleasure as O'Grady approached him. Shaking hands, the fellow apologized: I'm sorry to have kept you waiting.

Apparently by common consent, although the direction had actually been chosen by Gunnar, they began to walk rapidly towards the east, against the tide of humanity that swarmed to the subway Moloch. Paul did not know whither they were bound or why they were going anywhere, but it was certainly more comfortable to walk than to stand still in the nipping air, especially as O'Grady had the manner of a person with a destination in view.

I'm delighted to meet you again, the ex-boiler-mender cheerfully volunteered. You know, I have two books of yours.

O, I didn't give a damn about the books, Paul stammered, but I did want to find *you.* I've tried every way I could think of to get in touch with you. I've even advertised in the papers. He grinned.

O'Grady returned the grin but it was confused on his face with an expression of astonishment. Why, he declared, I would have come back. You should have known that. I had to return the books. I wanted to look them over, and I suddenly remembered an engagement, and you were away so long—I might have left a note.

You didn't leave anything except a trail of unsatisfied curiosity.

Still curious? Well, this is a happy ending. Come home with *me* this time.

Where do you live? They were moving in the general direction of Chatham Square.

Uptown. East Twenty-seventh Street. I wanted to get out of the crowd. It's easier walking this way.

You don't intend to walk home! Paul protested.

Why not? I always do. It hardens the muscles and sends the blood spinning through your veins. . . but if you want to ride. . .

I've walked so much today already, Paul explained.

You can't walk too much, O'Grady rejoined sternly, but he paused to hail a passing taxi, in the grand manner, Paul was interested to observe, of a Venetian gallant requisitioning a gondolier in a drawing by Longhi.

Once installed, Paul sighed with relief, offered Gunnar a cigarette which the fellow gently rejected, and lighted one for himself. This, he reflected, was the perfect ending of a chaotic, maudlin day. He felt very tired.

We didn't finish our conversation, he put forward as an excuse for opening another.

Nobody ever did finish a conversation, Gunnar replied. His high spirits seemed tralatitiously to lift the roof off the moving vehicle. It's impossible to do that. There's always so much more to say. Hamlet would be talking yet if Shakespeare hadn't killed him. Conversations are only concluded arbitrarily. The novelist brings a conversation to a full stop by surprisingly closing a chapter or by introducing the character of Death. It's the same in life. Conversations are only interrupted; they are never concluded.

Paul paid no attention to the sense of this harangue. I want to know, he persisted, why you were working as a furnace-mender, and why you quit. The boss of the company told me he would be willing to pay you double. He said you were the most efficient workman he had ever engaged.

So you went around there to look me up! Gunnar's wonderment increased.

That's nothing. I have been looking you up ever so many places. I don't think I should have stopped looking for you until I discovered you. I was lucky, that's that. But it's all so queer. Today I find you engaged in another unlikely occupation, and I suppose tomorrow. . . Well, what are you going to do tomorrow? It's none of my business, perhaps, but. . .

Everything is everybody's business, O'Grady asserted solemnly, only you've got to make it *your* business and not mere vulgar curiosity in some one else's. Why, every woman should be interested when another woman bears a child, because she should feel impelled to learn how to do it herself in the most efficient way, but if a woman is only interested in childbirth in relation to the question as to whether the offspring is by-blow or legitimate, then there's something wrong with her. He shook his head ominously.

But I don't get you yet! Paul cried. You seem to have discovered a philosophy of life or a mode of living that makes you happy, or healthy, or at least amuses you, and perhaps it would have this effect on me too, if I understood it. Perhaps, it would become my business.

It certainly is your business, his companion replied heartily.

Then explain it!

What do you want me to do? O'Grady questioned him sadly, peering at the same time out into the steel-blue atmosphere, splashed with the warm glow of the street-lamps. A feeble voice in the distance could be heard calling, Sex Weekly! Sex Weekly! . . . Shall I, Gunnar went on after a pause, take a chair at Columbia? I have already informed you that I am no preacher or professor. . . His air became even more serious. . . Nor would it do you any good if I were. You can't spread good tidings by talking. Why, Margaret Sanger has actually turned a great many people against birth-control, and William Jennings Bryan has probably interested a great many people in drinking, and John Roach Straton and John Sumner are excellent guides to the pseudo-vices, and the Republicans make men good Democrats, and the Democrats make men good Republicans. No, you can't disseminate a philosophy by vaunting its efficacy. Sometimes—his gaze was now full on Paul—you might do a good deal by just acting, living your life, and maintaining a strict silence in regard to it. That might interest a few. Or you might warn your potential disciples *not* to live the way you did; if you had faith in your manner of living, that might reasonably be better. But preach? *Never!*

Paul relinquished the siege. I think, perhaps, he admitted, that you are right.

Right! Nobody is ever right! I haven't pretended that I was right! I haven't said anything that had any right or wrong to it! Right! That would be preaching. I was merely conversing.

Then there's more? Paul brightened.

More! Enough to keep us busy talking through the ages!

Paul mentally noted that apparently there was a superior method, to that which involved interrogation, of getting under this fellow's conception of existence, an alternate approach to an eventual comprehension. In what exactly this method consisted O'Grady had not as yet made clear, but patience was essential in any real adventure, and his present experience seemed to Paul as clear-cut an example of adventure as any substitute that his not too fertile imagination was capable of conceiving.

Silence fell between them now, as the taxi-driver pursued his skilful route, threading dextrously in and out among the heavy motor-trucks and limousines that moved aimfully up and down the narrow thoroughfares they were traversing, and when he turned, artfully avoiding the wrong one-way streets. O'Grady was again gazing out of the window, and Paul followed his example, occasionally varying the monotony of this procedure by leaning back and exhaling cigarette smoke in a lazy manner, until, at last, the taxi stopped.

Here we are! Gunnar cried. They had halted before an old factory or office-building, the ground floor of which was occupied by a dealer in secondhand household goods, who esteemed his stock sufficiently so that he had caused to be painted across the window: Andrew Malony: Dealer in Antiques. In the midst of the jumble of old rugs, bronze statues, tabourets, fake majolica, and mahogany chairs, upholstered in rep, which cluttered the space behind the glass, Paul descried a desk, an excellent example of Chippendale, which afforded him an additional reason for memorizing the address.

They mounted the stairs, unlighted at this hour, save by a single jet of gas burning on the first landing, O'Grady swiftly darting up ahead through the gloom, shouting down when he had gone too far in advance, It's safe enough if you're familiar with it. Take your time if you want to, but you won't stumble. There's nothing to stumble over. Five flights had been ascended in this crazy fashion, O'Grady alternately flying ahead and then waiting until his more meticulous companion had made up the intervening distance, when Paul's eyes were solaced by a line of light glimmering under a door on the landing in front of him. O'Grady was already assaulting this portal with lusty blows. It was soon opened wide and Paul stood facing a man with superb physical development, his bare, muscular arms protruding from the openings in his gymnasium shirt, his legs encased in white flannel trousers.

Robin, O'Grady cried, I've brought a friend. You don't mind, do you?

I should say not. The stranger's voice was cordial. Come in! Come in!

Accepting this invitation, Paul was immediately presented to Robin and Hugo, the Brothers Steel, Gunnar explained, and then to Mrs. Hugo.

The four-winkled room, which extended half the depth of the loft, appeared to be utilized for all the domestic and professional rites performed by this curious quartet. At first view, with its silver trapezes swung on white ropes from beams in the high ceiling, its horizontal bars, its horses, its punching bags, its flying rings, its dumb-bells and Indian clubs, its padded mats, the chamber appeared to be a gymnasium, but gradually, in the shadows—the room was illuminated solely by gas-fixtures set in the wall, two on each side—Paul discerned a pair of cots, neatly made up—there was space for another bed behind a curtained recess—a broad rectangular table of unpainted pine, round which stools were arranged, a cook-stove, warmed for action, on which pots were steaming and away from the immediate vicinity of which it was distinctly chilly, and a cupboard or two, one open, displaying shelves neatly piled with plates and bowls and cups and saucers. On a clothes-line extending across a corner, from one wall to that which joined it at right angles, several sets of costumes were drying, tights and shirts of sky-blue, bright pink, and red, while the trunks which completed these outfits, lemon, black, and cerise satin, tricked out with tinsel gewgaws and bows of ribbons of the same shades, were heaped on the broad flat top of a dresser, where also reposed a loaf of bread in an envelope of glazed tissue, and a yellow bowl, harbouring apples and oranges.

The inmates, Paul fancied, were even odder than the room. Robin and Hugo, dressed precisely alike, also bore such an astonishing resemblance one to the other, that it was not difficult to come to the conclusion that they must be twins. Their rosy faces were round, their eyes soft and melting. Both flaunted bushy, black moustaches which would have given less naïve countenances an expression of the wildest ferocity but which, in the case of the Brothers Steel, simply seemed to be an incongruous detail. Both had parted their hair in an eccentrically barbered style with a mound of curls brushed carefully up over the right brow. The woman was not pretty, but her face was good-natured and pleasant—she reminded Paul of a little Roumanian dress-maker who had worked for Vera—and her plain serge frock was almost completely concealed under a blue and white striped apron. These details Paul was able to take in during his first fifteen minutes in this novel environment.

Well, boys, O'Grady cried out lustily from the curtained recess, where he was changing his clothes, how about a little exercise?

We ain't feelin' so good, Robin volunteered.

Nothin' extra, Hugo groaned.

You two sick! Impossible! O'Grady urged.

No, we ain't sick, Robin admitted.

Except to heart, was Hugo's amendment.

What's the matter? O'Grady demanded.

We don't know as your friend'd be interested.

Paul made an effort to dispel this mistaken point of view.

It's this way, Robin began, as Gunnar, clad in gymnasium togs similar to those worn by the brothers, emerged from behind the concealing curtain; layin' off this week on account o' no bookin' till next week when we go back on big time agin, we thought 'twouldn't do no harm to give a few acts the once over.

So, put in Hugo, we was to the Palace.

To see, Mrs. Hugo continued, that new act o' the Samson Family.

We didn't go to crib nothin'. Robin again was speaking. You know we ain't that kind. We always lived a good, clean, Christian life, tendin' our own personal business, and ain't never tried to pinch no novelties from outside artists.

We are—we always been—originators and innovators, Hugo announced proudly.

That's the way we always been billed, declared Mrs. Hugo, who, although not a member of the act, always spoke of it as We.

I know that, O'Grady averred sympathetically.

Well, you could a knocked us down, Robin moaned.

They copped our double backhand spring and return, Hugo explained.

That's the climax of your act! Gunnar cried excitedly.

The same. Now you know we ain't no more like the Samsons than soup's like wild honey. We're honest, clean professionals. Well, we tried that new stunt last week on the Pantages.

I told Robin we hadn't oughter done it, Hugo interpolated. I was for savin' it till we opened on big time.

You was right, his brother admitted from the lownesses of despair. Well, the Samsons was out front at Norfolk and they trimmed us. We ain't got nothin' new for big time now.

How about that balance stunt? O'Grady proffered the substitute.

Good, but not enough class, not enough pep. That's a nice quiet turn, but it ain't flashy enough for a finish. You gotta get their hands at the close. They'd be no healthy bend after that. They'd give us the raspberry. That double backhand spring and return was a wow!

It ain't strong enough, Hugo corroborated. How they got up in that double backhand spring and return so quick I can't figure out.

It's a shame, boys. Gunnar attempted to pacify them. Then, by way of encouragement, Show Moody what it is.

The Brothers Steel who had been sitting together on a bench, bowed statues of dejection, now called upon to excercise their agility, assumed at once a professional manner. Rising and expanding their chests, they ran to the edge of the mat, simultaneously lifting their right arms vertically over their heads. Retiring to the centre of the mat, Robin caught his brother by the right hand and, apparently without resorting to the use of strength, hoisted him to a standing posture on his shoulders. Robin now took a few rapid steps backwards and forwards to gain a perfect poise while Hugo skilfully balanced himself. Presently, with a cry of Allez houpla! Hugo sprang backwards, curling himself into the semblance of a ball which circled twice, landed on his feet, doubled under, and by some miracle of nimbleness projected himself back to his starting point. The feat was accomplished with as much skill and grace as Busoni would put into the performance of a Bach fugue. Paul was overcome by amazement and admiration.

Bravo! he cried.

Mrs. Hugo, occupied before the stove, preparing supper, turned, flushing with pleasure.

The Samsons can't do it like that, she announced. You know they're all wet.

Apple-sauce, Hugo rejoined. It don't matter how they do it. What matters is they done it. He assumed once more his non-professional air of dejection.

Well, cheer up, my lads, O'Grady urged. You'll have to think up a new one.

Yes, that's it! Robin echoed doubtfully. We gotta think of a new one.

We only got three days, Hugo deplored.

That's time enough, Gunnar declared. Come on, boys. Let's get to work.

Paul, more and more astonished, a picture of bright wonderment, indeed, now completely out of the scene, except as a spectator, sank into a chair and watched the manœuvres. Not altogether to his surprise, perhaps, for he had already received sufficient evidence regarding O'Grady's versatile prowess so that the successful accomplishment of anything that young man might have attempted would not have astonished him too much, Gunnar signalled his entrance into the practice of his comrades by a spring across the mat, followed by a couple of light aerial somersaults. Thereafter, the three bodies were consecrated to intricate forms of movement, to which the gymnasts had so adjusted their capabilities that they invested the most hazardous evolutions with an appearance of simplicity. Sometimes all three appeared to soar in the air together; sometimes two lay on their backs, legs in air, like Japanese jugglers, while the third, apparently in a state of catalepsy, was kicked back and forth; sometimes they rose like a tower, the higher men's feet on the lower men's shoulders, only to make this pose the basis of a furious and complicated operation. Their finesse, their electric energy, their defiance of the laws of gravity, all won the ready eye and enthusiasm of Paul. He had, to be sure, witnessed the exploits of acrobats before, but never before such paragons under such intimate conditions. It was, he reflected, like hearing Kreisler play in one's bedchamber before breakfast.

In conclusion, the athletes formed a huge human hoop which rolled off the mat and down the length of the hall.

Supper's ready, Mrs. Hugo called out.

All right, mother.

You'll stay, Mr. Moody?

I. . .

Of course, you'll stay, O'Grady shouted. What do you think I brought you here for?

Course he'll stay, echoed Hugo and Robin. The three took turns at dousing their faces and arms with cold water at a sink in one corner of the room.

I'd like to, Paul declared, if you don't mind.

There's always enough for five, Mrs. Hugo promised him.

The group gathered around the table. The acrobats had drawn bathrobes about their heated bodies. Their faces were shiny. They even looked happier.

I'll tell you what it is, Hugo began, forking a steaming potato, you gotta go into the act next week, Gunnar.

Robin's mouth was full of stew, but he sputtered out a You bet!

But I'm just learning the profession, the young man protested.

Apple-sauce. You're better 'an we are now. Ain't he, mother?

Well, he's just as good.

There! cried Hugo. D'ya hear that? That means a whole lot from the little woman. She ain't the one to never say no more'n that.

What do you think? Gunnar demanded of Paul.

I think you can do anything! Paul cried. Why. . .

Gunnar signalled him a mute plea for silence.

Well, he considered aloud, I was going to some day. Why not next week? Where do you play?

We're billed at the Riverside. We close the show.

It takes a good act, Robin explained to Paul, to close the show and not have the customers walk out on you. Why, mother, he observed abruptly, there's peppers. I must feed Sophie Tucker. Impaling a pepper on a fork he carried it to a bird-cage which hung in a window. A canary fluttered to the bars. Robin held the pepper tantalizingly near to the beak of the bird, as he began to talk: Now, Sophie, d'ya want a pepper? Well, ask for it right. The fluttering canary began a prodigious twittering. Robin projected his lips until they touched the bars of the cage. Kiss me, Sophie, he begged. The bird flew back to her perch. Kiss me! Kiss me! he insisted. Returning, Sophie lightly pecked Robin's lips. There! Now you can have your pepper. Opening the door he dropped it into the cage.

We gotta work hard, Hugo remarked, as his brother returned to the table. We gotta practise every day for speed.

We oughter get more money for the act with three.

I don't want any salary, Gunnar cried out in dismay. I'm willing to go into this, but I refuse to accept payment.

Now see here, bo, Robin protested, you get one-third o' whatever we get. You're part o' the act from now on.

You work hard all day, said Hugo, and you been payin' us for stayin' here and learnin' the profession. It's only fair that you get one-third. It's only O. K., ain't it, mother?

Sure it's O. K.

Gunnar sighed. All right, boys, if you say so.

After dinner, while Mrs. Hugo washed the dishes and Robin dried them, Hugo produced an accordion and began to play, not modern jazz tunes, but sentimental ballads of an earlier day, Sweet Rosie O'Grady, The Sidewalks of New York, and The Belle of Avenue A. In a mood of reverie, Gunnar half-reclined beside Paul on a cot. When

Hugo broke into I've got rings on my fingers, bells on my toes, Robin began to sing, elephants to ride upon, my little Irish Rose. Paul, Gunnar requested, his voice covered by the music, don't tell them where you've seen me before. They don't know anything about me. I pay my way here. I study their art—yes, it is an art—and that's all they have to know.

Of course, I won't say a word, Paul assured him. I couldn't tell them very much about you, unless I made it up. I want to know more about you than they do. . . He had forgotten his decision to ask no more questions. . . I was curious enough when I first met you. Well, now my ears, eyes, and mouth are wide open. What does it all mean?

Gunnar gazed at him compassionately. You'll come again? he inquired.

I've got rings on my fingers and bells on my toes. . .

Will I? Rather! When?

Gunnar laughed at this burst of enthusiasm. If you don't mind, he suggested, wait until after my début. I'm not going back to Shidrowitz, but I've got to work hard here. I must do my part to put the team over. He laughed louder. It's funny when you think of it, he explained. The manager engaged two brothers, and he's getting three! Elephants to ride upon. . . I say! Will you come to see me perform?

I'll be at the Riverside Monday afternoon.

And after that whenever you like, if you like. Do you understand any better?

I'll be damned if I do, but it doesn't matter. It's interesting enough without understanding.

Gunnar rose from the couch. Paul noted to his amazement that tears glistened in the corners of the young man's eyes.

I had almost forgotten the books, he said.

O, keep them! Paul urged, with a brusqueness born of embarrassment.

Five

In her own room Campaspe could always find repose and a satisfactory background for the variety of reflection which was her only serious form of self-indulgence. On this winter morning reclining on her chaise longue of white horse-hair, edged with vermilion, before the cheer of her grate-fire, she was unaware, apparently, for the heavy turquoise-blue curtains were drawn across the windows and the room was artificially illuminated, that slivers of sleet flung themselves across the street, like silver ribbons scattered by merry-makers at a carnival, and that heavy, low-hanging clouds masked the sky, giving it the appearance of a vast cathedral dome, painted by some cinquecento artist, of which the colours had dimmed and dulled in the passage of the years. Campaspe, indeed, engaged in plucking her eyebrows in this little chamber which retained only the pictures and bric-à-brac and bibelots to which she was warmly attached or newly drawn or entirely oblivious, was as isolated as Tut-Ankh-Amen in the sealed seclusion of his tomb, with the important distinction that, unlike the mummified emperor, she was alertly sentient, her agile mind hopping from one theme to another, as a bird might hop from branch to branch on a favourite tree.

To Campaspe, then, with the rich resources of her imagination constantly at her command, there existed slight possibility of dulness. There might spread before her fallow periods in which nothing, of the many external actions and accidents that served to capture her willing attention, occurred, but it was during these periods that she took occasion to put her mental house in order, to shake out of her brain whatever lingering superstitions or inhibitions had come to her like trailing clouds of responsibility out of the dark backward and abysm of time.

She was aware of a distinct sensation that she had returned to a New York which was a little different from the New York to which she had become accustomed during the years immediately succeeding the war. People were tiring of one another, tiring of themselves, tiring of doing the same thing. Deeds of violence were prevalent, vicious tongues more active: the world had nerves again, nerves and problems, a state of affairs which she had once been simple enough to believe the war had exhausted for all time. It was curious to find even placid Laura facing a problem, and Campaspe wondered, half-amused, if Laura would consult a psychanalyst regarding her enigma, as was the current fashion, rather than a priest. Laura, who had always played so safe, had, it appeared, hatched an ugly duckling, morally ugly, at any rate from Laura's limited point of view. Campaspe considered what she herself would do with Consuelo, and with no difficulty extracted the answer from her consciousness: she would do nothing at all. With her there would have been no problem in connection with the rearing of an unusual daughter; she would have reared her as she had brought up her own two conventional and conservative sons, by permitting her, within limits prescribed by Campaspe's own comfort, to bring up herself. This, the musing lady assured herself, Laura would never do, and so the duckling eventually, she shrewdly guessed, would cackle or bleat, or whatever ducklings did, out of Laura's jurisdiction. The duckling, already, it would seem, had developed sufficient initiative to pick up a paragon in a flower-shop. God knows, Campaspe added to herself, what train of amusing circumstances might have followed had we rediscovered him. The unsuccessful outcome of that adventure, however, did not present itself to her in retrospect as entirely unfortunate. Basil, for one thing, would have proved a disturbing presence, disturbing in his passive acceptance of whatever might have occurred, and now Basil, after his few necessary days in town, had been packed off to school again. In spite of this reasonable resignation in regard to the inevitable, Campaspe could not deny that her failure to encounter O'Grady had annoyed her considerably at the time, but she realized vividly, in compensation, that sooner or later he would certainly stray across her path in a manner potentially more amusing than that which the atmosphere of a flower-shop might be depended upon to provide.

Paul was an even more alluring subject for study than Laura, for Laura, after all, only presented the eternally recurring spectacle of tradition confronted by change, but Campaspe could conceive no adequate reason why Paul should not have settled back into his own comfortable, pagan self after his marriage with the extremely rich, if somewhat pinguid, Vera Whittaker. She could only explain his recent moods by recourse to her theory of nerves, and it had not occurred to her before now that Paul was a prey to nerves. He did not, to be sure, seem exactly irritable—that state was reserved for the fair Vera—but he did seem more intense, more bored, and less, Campaspe judged, interesting, unless, perchance, this boiler-mender had produced some subtle metamorphosis in Paul which would again give him at least the validity of a mural decoration to repay the onlooker's casual glance, if, indeed, not the closer inspection of the collector on the lookout for a true Orcagna.

At this point in her meditation Campaspe's eye roved to the wall opposite, a wall on which were hanging three new pictures by a young Jew, Issachar Ber Rybbak, in which she recognized a kind of inspiration which aroused her appreciation more abundantly than any other paintings had succeeded in doing since she had first seen the work of Chagall. There was a breadth of design, a sombre humour, a disquieting power of observation tinged with fancy, in these representations of goats lying in tortured streets, these lusty rabbis making merry with wine on Simchath Torah, these withering crones knitting in the picturesque surroundings created by a perfect bad taste, which captured and held her complete attention, and which compelled the expression, to herself at any rate, of her increasingly gratified admiration. They were, she was happy to admit, possessing them, as good as anything of the kind could ever be. . .

Her eyes did not stray from the canvases for some time. At last, however, she turned to the table beside her and idly sought the morning post. There was, certainly, no letter from Fannie. Since she had married Manfred Cohen, Mrs. Lorillard's mother's penchant for wandering had increased. She and her husband, as a matter of fact, were at present enjoying a leisurely journey around the world. Postcards occasionally arrived from Benares or Luxor or Pekin, but they had no more to announce than, I hope you are as happy as I am, or some kindred sentiment. Today there was not even a postcard. To offset this lack there was a letter from Edith Dale, who seemed content to remain indefinitely in the rambling, Spanish house she had built for herself on a plateau in New Mexico, and an envelope addressed in a hand which Campaspe did not immediately recognize. For the moment, she passed these by to open a third envelope which she suspected of containing an advertisement, a species of printed epistle which she was seldom able to resist in the matter of precedence. Tearing open the flap, therefore, she drew out a card from Mrs. Humphry Pollanger, inviting her to attend an evening entertainment given in honour of Gareth Johns, the American novelist who, after an extended sojourn in Europe, had recently returned to his native land. A reinspection of the envelope exhibited a characteristic idiosyncrasy of Mrs. Pollanger, her use of the black and grey seven cent stamp with its portrait of McKinley, because of its dignity and sobriety and the further important fact that it harmonized with the mauve of her stationery, a certain clue to the identity of the sender which Campaspe had missed in her first glance. Opening the other letter from an as yet unidentified correspondent, she was amazed to discover that it was signed Ella Nattatorrini. Campaspe smiled as she noted the coincidence of the juxtaposed envelopes, recalling the events which had occurred in a suite at the Hotel Bristol in the Place Vendôme, on an afternoon ever so long ago, when she had thoroughly learned the meaning of that stock phrase, "dissolved in tears." The Countess, indeed, improving on Niobe's original performance, had shrieked while the process was in accomplishment. The long, sordid story—or at least as much of it as Ella cared to remember, which was considerable—had been retailed, and Campaspe found it simple to bring it back to mind now, in its general effect, if not in its details, although, at the time, it had not seemed to be anything more than the usual history of love and disillusion, complicated, to be sure, with an unbelievable amount of repetition. At this point in her reverie she found it expedient to consult the Countess's note, discovering therein that Madame Nattatorrini, after an absence of twenty-seven years, was returning to America, a strange decision, Campaspe reflected, for a woman who must be seventy-six or seventy-seven to make. The letter, the first Campaspe had ever received from the Countess, was formal in style and scrawled in that dispiriting chirography which betokens the palsied hand of the aged.

This, then, was the Nemesis of the Greeks, acting again in modern times: the Countess and Gareth were to meet, figuratively speaking, at least, in New York, after the lapse of twenty-seven years, after, moreover, the publication of Gareth Johns's latest novel, Two on the Seine, which, like Il Fuoco, tore away the veils from the soul of a silly woman in her middle years with an unrequited passion for a young boy. Considering these matters, Campaspe assured herself that her fallow period was at an end, if, indeed, it could be said ever really to have begun. . .

She lifted Edith Dale's letter. It was very long and she skimmed a page or two before the lines held her attention. Then: Magdalen Roberts has hit upon a certain secret we all know and is going to teach it for large sums of money. Her little tract is called The Importance of the Façade. Have you seen it? She writes in a learned way of the basic principle of facial integrity—in which she proposes to give instruction, though she admits it will be expensive, but worth the money. In fact, she is going to show her students how to make faces! Of course, any meditative person like you or me learns from our own insides how to make our faces. We're the kind who find out *all* our secrets. A few others know this trick. I once knew a man who was as dissipated and drunk-ridden as it was possible to be, but he cared for just one thing more than drink and that was his beautiful face. He put his attention on it and kept it intact. He knew how to renew it daily from the source—and how to wipe off every blemish. One would see him coming to lunch around the corner of the house—unaware of observers—and the ghastly reaction of drink pressure criss-crossed his face and everything sagged and puffed, but once in the door, the creator had wiped off every trace and the Greek mask prevailed. We can all do this if we learn how and *want* to badly enough. And furthermore we can do it *when* we want to—and when we don't want to our faces go hang with their lines of least resistance—but we can assume them again at *any moment*. We can be twenty at one hour and sixty the next. And all this Magdalen Roberts is going to tell for money: the gentle art of making faces! . . . Campaspe smiled as she skipped a page or two. . . Edith appeared to be writing about that strange, Spanish sect of flagilants, the Penitentes. She stood in the Church of the Marada. We peeked into an inner chapel, so the letter continued, and caught a glimpse of the delightful place—white-washed walls so splotched with recent blood-splashing that they gave a dark impression—a little wagon with solid wooden wheels on which was seated a life-sized skeleton, laughing, bearing bow and arrow, the arrow poised, the bow drawn. On the floor were great heaps of shiny chains, that the Penitentes rattle as they sing and whip, and the curious instrument to drown the howls, which gives out a terrific sound like a Chinese rattle. We. . .

The telephone tinkled. Campaspe, after some argument with the telephone company, had contrived to have an English instrument installed, so that it was possible for her to grasp both receiver and transmitter in one hand without altering her half-recumbent position. Paulet was on the wire, Paulet in great excitement, Paulet with news, Paulet with the desire to lunch with her. Paulet in this mood was almost a forgotten experience for Campaspe. To her expert intelligence it was quite evident that he had rediscovered his furnace-man, although he had not said so.

THE PURPLE GLASS FRUIT-PLATES, CONTAINING oranges preserved in grenadine, rested on the maple board before Paul had done with the relation of his incredible history. As she listened to the peroration Campaspe automatically made a pretence of cutting into the dyed rind of the pungent fruit. Her eyes, however, did not stray from the face of her companion.

He wound up with a query. What, if any, do you make of it, 'paspe?

Mrs. Lorillard supported her chin on her right palm and appeared to meditate. What was really running through her mind was something like this: In completely esoteric situations it is wise to reject obvious explanations, at any rate wise to come to no definite conclusions, until one has been vouchsafed the opportunity to form a first-hand impression.

I think, she declared aloud, that I shall give a box-party at the Riverside Monday afternoon. Whom shall I ask?

Why don't we go alone?

No. . . Campaspe appeared to be considering. . . I don't think so. Consuelo. . .

Consuelo!

You are not aware, perhaps, that Consuelo has also struck up an acquaintance with this young man of irregular customs.

If it's the chap she met at the florist's, Vera told me something.

It is, I believe you will discover, the same. At any rate, we shan't know unless we take Consuelo with us. I think I shall invite Vera, too.

Vera! Paul groaned.

Now, Paulet, you must learn to be more sympathetic with Vera. You're not playing the game. You don't want to go back to your flat in Gramercy Park, do you?

Some days I think I'd like to.

Campaspe regarded this friend of long standing with something approaching consternation. What had come over him? What was the cause of this eclipse of his usually blithe spirit? Well, it would serve no purpose to inquire. As was her happy way, she bided her time.

But you haven't answered my question, 'paspe, Paul persisted. What do you think this boy's up to?

Paulet, she mock-chided him, you appear to regard this serious matter as if it were merely a cross-word puzzle.

It gets me! he exclaimed. I'm eaten up with curiosity. I'm inquisitive and, at the same time, I half-sense something. 'paspe, he blurted out, regarding her almost shamefacedly. . . I'm going to work.

Going to work!

Yes, he hurried on, I've got to do something. I'm not satisfied. My life is too empty.

Reflect, Paulet, reflect ere you make this decision. Campaspe's face was wreathed in a series of ironic smiles, subtly blending one with the other.

Paul remained silent, even grave.

What do you intend to do? Campaspe attempted to demand with more seriousness.

I thought, perhaps. . . there were strangely uncharacteristic breaks between the words. . . Cupid might take me in. He must have loads of jobs in his brokering place.

It's quite possible. I'll ask him.

You'll do that, 'paspe!

Of course. Don't be an ass, Paulet. Of course, I'll do that. More and more, as she observed this butterfly of long acquaintance turning back into a chrysalis, she was puzzled and amazed. Only try to think, Paulet. . . she tasted her orange to give her query a more casual air. . . is it O'Grady who has put you up to this, or just your life with Vera?

Damned if I know, 'paspe. I think I was bored, but I saw no way out. Then I met O'Grady. He seemed to be having such a jolly time working, working at such tough jobs, too. There's something about him—you'll feel it yourself when you know him—that convinces you that he's happy straight through. It's queer, the whole thing—you know I can't explain anything very well. I thought *you'd* explain it, he concluded lamely.

Campaspe seldom permitted her cynicism to colour her tone. She uttered the following phrase in a voice instinct with the deepest charm: Paulet, you're exactly like Tyltyl searching for that blue fowl.

Now, 'paspe, don't be rough! He held up a protesting hand.

She did not spare him: I shall have to begin to call you Paulianna.

He grinned. I know I'm ridiculous, he admitted.

Anyhow, here is your coffee.

Thanks. He accepted the cup. You'll see for yourself, he went on defiantly, and O, God! 'paspe, Vera's so dull.

HAD MRS. LORILLARD NEEDED ANY ADDITIONAL evidence in regard to the truth of this latter dictum, she received it later in the afternoon. With her drawing-room crowded with what she called her time-fillers, men and women of Laura's set whom she permitted to visit her occasionally, Vera Moody was announced. The appearance in the doorway of stout Vera, her curved figure expensively upholstered in black velvet and bundled in furs, her bosom festooned with pearls, her eyes circled by a betraying red, was a signal for Campaspe to invent a suitable excuse to rid herself of her other callers, not a particularly difficult feat for a woman with her superior cunning.

Once they shared the room between them the fat lady poured out her pangs without reserve.

Paul, she sobbed, doesn't love me any more.

Nonsense, Vera! What's the matter? Campaspe invariably treated the erstwhile Mrs. Whittaker with a considerable degree of brusque impatience. This served not only to soothe her own nerves but also to cow Vera into a state of complete release.

He says. . . Mrs. Moody's voice now rose to a shrill wail. . . that he's going to work!

Is that what you're making all this fuss about? He told me as much today.

Was he here today? The lady seemed to hover on the verge of another explosion which, taking into consideration her proportions, suggested that it would have about enough force to complete the demolition of Rheims Cathedral.

Certainly. He had luncheon with me.

He never lunches with me any more, Mrs. Moody whimpered, and last night he dined out again. But I don't mind that. I know you're one of his *oldest* friends. It's his going to work that kills me.

I promised to speak to Cupid about getting him a position. Mrs. Lorillard absent-mindedly began to whistle.

Campaspe, you wouldn't do that!

I don't see why not. If he wants to go to work, let him.

Campaspe, don't you see? Can't you understand? It's a reflection on me. It means he's tired of me. Why should he want to work otherwise? I've got plenty of money. Why won't he continue to allow me take care of him as I have in the past? He's tired of me! I know he's tired of me!

Campaspe smiled, the more readily as the woman's calloidal convulsions reminded her of the shivering of a mammoth platter of jelly. If I were you, she suggested, I shouldn't worry about Paul's latest decision. He has only threatened to go to work; he hasn't agreed to support himself. He certainly will not succeed in doing so in Cupid's office. Cupid is notoriously close in his business relations.

O, do you think. . . ? Vera brightened a little, but her handkerchief was black with the mascara which had rubbed off her lashes, and the dark tears flowed from her smarting eyes.

I know, Campaspe averred. Let him go to work. It won't do him any harm, I suppose. You see, he has a problem to solve.

It's that furnace-man! Vera spoke with as much bitter vehemence as it was possible for her to summon from her plump, good-natured depths. Ever since he came into the house everything has been different.

Paulet says he's curious.

Curious! Vera cried. I should think he is. He's reading books on the uplift, Swedenborg and Freud. I've never before known him to take any interest in subjects like that.

Has he, Campaspe demanded, fascinated, read In Tune with the Infinite?

I don't know. I can't remember all the titles, but his library is beginning to look like Mrs. Pollanger's does on the day before she gives one of those talks of hers at the Woman's Club.

Well, Vera, dry those idle tears. Campaspe began to feel a strong desire to put an end to this scene. He won't go to work until after Monday anyway. I'm giving a box-party at the Riverside on the afternoon of that day. Paulet has promised to be present, and I want you to come, too.

Well, that *is* nice of you, Campaspe, Mrs. Moody, now completely mollified, gurgled. You usually prefer to be alone, you and Paul, you have so much to talk about. Vera opened her cornelian compact and powdered her nose.

You'll come? Campaspe queried grimly.

Of course, Vera replied. As she rose to take her departure, one of the strands of pearls caught under the arm of her chair. The tension caused the chain to break, scattering the iridescent bubbles over the rug.

Six

Consuelo sat very quiet, her slender legs dangling over the edge of the couch.

Of course, it is with Campaspe, Laura was qualifying, and it would probably be all right this time. There's certainly no harm in her attending a vaudeville entertainment, except for the fact that she is going out altogether too much. She's acquiring, Laura concluded darkly, too many ideas.

Consuelo's face was pale and emotionless. One could hardly be sure that she was listening at all to this family discussion conducted insensitively without regard for her presence, notwithstanding the certainty that she herself provided the theme for it.

I can't imagine where she gets them all, Laura wailed.

Perhaps, George suggested, from her governess.

No, George. . . Laura spoke decisively. . . I am sure they do not come from Miss Pinchon. I have the utmost faith in her conservatism. I think it must be from books. Consuelo, dear, why aren't you like other little girls?

Directly addressed, the child replied, although without altering her position and apparently without any special interest, I don't profess to have the slightest idea, maman, what other little girls may be like. I must admit that I don't understand them at all. I only know that they're not in the least like me.

She complained of a headache and excused herself from the dance Mrs. Nicander gave for the children last week, after she had been there five minutes, Laura continued.

Well, maman, frankly I was bored.

But Consuelo dear, you don't even appear to be interested in your home and your mama and papa and sister.

I'm sorry, maman. I'm fond of you all—in a way—and I know you do all you can—that is everything you know how to do—to make it pleasant for me, but you will acknowledge that the conversation in this house is on a pretty inferior plane.

George turned aside and blew his nose violently. Laura gasped, and gave the impression—opening and closing her mouth rapidly several times—that she was about to make some drastic comment. Apparently, she altered her original intention, for her lips eventually formed these words instead, Consuelo dear, you may certainly accompany Mrs. Lorillard to the Riverside, and now run away. Papa and I want to talk.

Slowly, the child slid down from the couch until her feet touched the floor. Then rising, with great dignity she retired from the room, first casting her mother one of the most subdolous in her extensive repertory of glances, any one of which was calculated to puzzle and disquiet Laura for several hours after she had received it.

As Consuelo, with a great show of courtesy, closed the door carefully behind her, Laura demanded, Did you hear that?

George was laughing. Of course, I heard it, Laura. By Jove, the kid's a wonder. I never thought I'd live to be jacked up by my own child about the tone of my conversation.

Laura was thoughtful. It isn't, she mused audibly, as if she were impolite. I don't think she is ever really that. Her governess reports that she is an angel so far as her deportment goes, but she has such a disconcerting habit of saying what she thinks, and she thinks so much!

Well, Laura, George suggested, I suppose the best thing to do, since she hasn't yet joined the Bolshevists or tried to set fire to the house, is to let her go right on thinking, even if she thinks out loud. That's the English system regarding free speech. In London they give radicals the opportunity to say anything they please publicly or privately, even to write it. This serves to let off a lot of steam and probably preserves the empire. People who talk seldom act. The Russian Tsars never learned that lesson and look where they are now. So long as Consuelo behaves herself to any reasonable degree, let her think or say what she wants to.

But George, Laura protested, we can't do that. She'd grow up a barbarian. She expresses the strangest, most mature ideas on every conceivable subject, subjects that I wouldn't dare allow my mind to dwell on, even yet. Why, when I was a girl. . .

I know, I know. George was becoming a trifle impatient. Times have changed, Laura. It's the younger generation.

I've read a good deal about this younger generation and these young intellectuals, but I've always understood that they were over ten.

We should be proud that we have raised a prodigy.

Laura perpended this statement. I think, she put forward, after a pause, that we should send her away to school.

George laughed again. Why, they wouldn't stand for that child in any school, he exclaimed. She'd corrupt the minds of all the other pupils. Besides, she'd never learn anything. She already knows more than any Yale graduate I ever met.

Then, what *are* we to do?

I think we'll just have to wait and see what happens, George counselled. Let's be patient. Leave the girl alone. Let her think, let her talk. You'll see: the family will be as stable as Britannia in the end. Don't make the Romanoff mistake of sending free-thinkers to Siberia. It never works.

You may be right, George, Laura assented, but her tone did not carry the ring of assurance.

Paul and Vera arrived at the Riverside shortly after three, just in time to observe a pair of comedians whacking each other frantically with folded newspapers. Vaudeville audiences, originally, had accepted this gesture as funny in itself. Now the humour lay in appreciating the fact that it had once been considered amusing. Paul had notified Campaspe that, as the Brothers Steel were announced to close the bill, she need not, therefore, present herself before four-thirty. He himself, however, had experienced apprehension lest there might be an inversion in the promised order of the program, which would bring on the acrobats before their appointed hour.

Vera was so delighted by the idea of being permitted to go out in the joint company of her husband and Campaspe that she gave the impression of resembling a stout bottle, so charged with soda, the bubbles constantly rising to the top to seek release, that it might explode at any moment.

I know we shall enjoy ourselves, she explained. I haven't been to a vaudeville show for ages.

Paul, too, was in an excellent, withal somewhat grave, mood. They settled themselves in the gilded cane ball-room chairs which furnished the box, with plaster cupids in amorous attitudes presiding symbolically in a great shell above their heads. Vera sought her husband's hand, and he did not withdraw it immediately.

I shall just die! Vera cackled. Did you hear what that man said?

Yes, I heard. Paul smiled.

An exhibition of trained seals followed the two comedians. These incipient coats caught rubber balls on their noses, played musical instruments, shot off revolvers, and waved American flags. After each of these feats they barked excitedly until their trainer, a young woman in high, white, Russian boots and a blue satin costume, edged around the bottom with polar bear fur, dropped her whip to toss them fish, which they caught in the air and devoured edaciously.

O, Paul, I'm having *such* a good time, Vera declared. Let's go out together oftener.

Whenever you like, Vera. . . Paul slowly withdrew his hand from the grasp of her palm. . . I think that seal is about to ride a bicycle.

Paul, Vera begged, and her manner had become coy and whimpering, please promise me something.

What is it, Vera?

Promise me you won't go to work.

I can't do that, Vera.

I don't think it's fair to me, Paul. Really, I don't. People will take it as a reflection on the way I treat you. I've done everything I could for you, Paul, but the cats will say you're not satisfied, that you want more. . . I'll give you more, she avowed wildly, anything you want!

You've been wonderful, Vera. It isn't that you haven't, he lied. God! This was worse than Amy!

Let me be wonderful to you—let me go on being, I mean. It makes me happy, Paul. I shall never be happy again if you go to work.

I'm sorry, Vera. The band was playing What'll I Do? to accompany the evolutions of the seals, but it sounded like incidental music for this conversation.

If you *really* loved me, you'd be content to let me support you. You don't love me any more. Vera was weeping, softly at first, but Paul was acquainted with her capacity for making a noise as soon as she truly began to enjoy her grief.

Of course, I do, he countered distractedly, and he was grateful at this moment to observe the name of Nora Bayes flash in the announcement frame. Vera chose the instant when the self-confident performer, screened by a preposterously enormous fan of orange feathers, undulated in the direction of the footlights to permit a sob of anguish to escape. As Paul had anticipated, however, this cry was drowned out by the power of sound expelled from the stage. The scene was further interrupted by the arrival of Campaspe and Consuelo. The former took in the situation at once, understood it, and ignored it, seating herself in the place reserved for her and, with a wave of the hand, inviting Consuelo to follow her example. The child was bundled in a cloak of white fox on which she had fastened a spray of brown and yellow orchids. Hesitating a little before she removed this outer covering and her gloves, she sat watching and listening intently to the entertainer on the stage.

She sings so loud: Consuelo explained the reason for her interest, as Miss Bayes retired to change her dress, while the pianist fingered through Chopin's Minute Waltz in a manner which reminded Campaspe of eggs boiling with the advice of a sand-glass. I never heard any one sing so loud before, the awed child continued, not even Rosa Ponselle or Jeritza.

You should hear Sophie Tucker or Eva Tanguay, Paul advised.

Do they sing louder?

Much louder.

I want to, the little girl averred with great simplicity, as she consulted her program.

Vera, whose display of mental anguish had created neither sympathy nor comment, began to dry her eyes. Long ago, Campaspe had learned that the proper manner of dealing with Vera's emotions was to disregard them, for if Vera discovered that she was not pleasing you in one way she immediately tried another. Vera's whole existence had been devoted to a vain effort to please somebody or other. It cannot be said that she ever quite succeeded even in pleasing herself.

Nora Bayes was interpreting another popular ditty.

I think she's very clever, Vera, who had now reassumed some semblance of a cheerful, social tone, informed her friends.

She uses her fan well, Campaspe tossed her.

Doesn't she? Vera gushed, grateful for this first slight attention.

It's almost as big as her voice, Consuelo piped up.

Campaspe arrided her. Quite, you delicious child! When do your friends come on, Paul?

They follow this number.

Then we arrived just in time.

Rather, too early. Bayes will sing for half-an-hour.

This apparently mantic prognostication proved to be entirely correct. Miss Bayes rendered song after song, and when, at last, she seemed willing to desist, the crowd in the theatre, by its exuberant applause, persuaded her to begin another, and another, and another. In the end, she made a little speech, kissed her hand, waved her fan in a final flourish, and disappeared from view. Even then, even, indeed, after the illuminated placard had signalled the appearance of the Brothers Steel: Acrobats, the clapping of hands persisted. As it seemed impossible, however, to drag the popular entertainer out again, a general exodus began, and the trio offered the opening moments of their act to an audience composed largely of retreating backs.

It's my O'Grady! Consuelo cried, and then, annoyed by the sound of retreating footsteps, Why are they all going away?

No one ever stays for the last act of a vaudeville bill, Paul explained, but he was as much put out as Consuelo.

Why not? the child demanded.

It's taken for granted it will be dull.

No longer interrupted by the stamping of outgoing feet, the little group in the box devoted their exclusive attention to the stage. The act began tamely enough, as is customary with acrobats, with a prodigious amount of saltatorial exercise, allez houplaing, and fumbling with handkerchiefs. As it continued, there was a crescendo in the difficulty of the feats. Campaspe had adjusted her lorgnette. Without asking for an identification, she recognized Gunnar at once. The brothers wore moustaches and their hair was piled in a ridiculous fashion above their foreheads. O'Grady's hair was combed straight back and his face was clean shaven. And, although all three were dressed precisely alike in purple tights covering their bodies with the exception of the loins which were encased in indigo trunks, tricked out with gold ruchings and ribbons, she was immediately aware of still more subtle distinctions. It was evident, for instance, that O'Grady possessed a far superior skill to that of the Brothers Steel. Not only did he perform his part in the intricate manœuvres with consummate dexterity, but also there was a rhythm in his movement, a *continuity* which, Campaspe reflected, she had never before witnessed save in the dancing of Nijinsky. And there was still something else. . .

Isn't he lovely! Consuelo cried.

The act continued in all its familiar routine, including the swift run of the performers to the footlights, with the terminal raising of the right arm, a traditional gesture which has persisted since the days of the Roman circus, even when there is no public enthusiasm to encourage it. On this occasion, assuredly, there was very little enthusiasm. Not only did the Brothers Steel occupy the final position on the bill, but also they were acrobats. Ignominy in vaudeville could scarcely sink to a lower level. Individual spectators continued to file out, and the theatre was nearly empty when the brothers were going through their last evolutions, in complicated mazes of pleached arms and legs. These, at length, came to an end and the curtain fell, nor did it rise again in response to the faint championship, most of which was contributed by the tiny hands and inadequate physical force of Consuelo. Then, abruptly, to the accompaniment of a jolly tune by George Gershwin, the asbestos curtain was lowered.

It's over, Consuelo sighed.

It was very nice, Vera conceded, very. Still, Miss Bayes. . .

Shall we go back? Paul demanded, hoping they would refuse.

. . . is certainly an artist.

Naturally, Campaspe replied to Paul.

Naturally, was Consuelo's psittaceous comment.

Shall I wait for you, Paul dear? Vera inquired tremulously.

Certainly not, her husband growled. Come along.

At the stage-door, however, they were halted by a human hulk, with a black cigar between its teeth, which informed them that never, by no means, I should say not, could they set foot inside the theatre. As a concession to their obviously plausible appearance he was good enough to add, Rules.

But why? Campaspe insisted. What are the rules for?

Say! Where d'ya tink y'are? At de Bee-lasco? Why? Cause yer might be a heel from de Police Gazette back here to pick up de low-down, or yer might be. . . Say! How de hell do I know who y'are?

Why, the idea! Vera cried, giggling nervously.

Well, we'll wait for him here, Campaspe decided, the weather being propitious enough to make this possible, and she pointed to a long, wooden bench against the wall, on a board above which had been pasted advertisements of and testimonials to various teams and acts. Presently Nora Bayes emerged, a dog in her arms and a coloured maid at her heels. She devoted more than a passing glance to the curious quartet seated on the bench before she entered her car. Now the stage-hands were issuing from the guarded portal, and Consuelo listened to a number of novel words and phrases. Fortunately, her memory was excellent. And, at last, the Brothers Steel and O'Grady. Paul presented the trio to the quartet in one general introduction.

We flopped, Hugo complained.

We'll be back on Pantages next week, Robin sighed.

Nonsense! Gunnar encouraged them. It went all right.

At this moment Gunnar's stare met that of Campaspe and some kind of aberrant communication passed between the two.

Paul, who had not observed this pregnant phenomenon, was corroborating Gunnar's protestation. Vera, not a little thrilled in the presence of so many handsome young men, athletically inclined too, gurgled her enjoyment. Consuelo appeared to be somewhat reserved, even discomfited. Presently, she explained the cause of her annoyance. You don't recognize me! she declared.

Gunnar turned his eyes away from Campaspe to focus them on the child. He seemed to be strangely, and unreasonably, perturbed.

Why, of course, I do, he said. Then, in a whisper, They don't know, the Steels, about the florist. Don't tell them, will you?

Delighted to share a confidence, Consuelo gave him the requisite assurance. Then she inquired, When am I going to see you again?

Once more Gunnar looked at Campaspe as he replied, I don't know. He seemed troubled, even a little dazed. Campaspe had not yet spoken one word. Her eyes were hyaline. Paul was chatting with the brothers. Suddenly, without warning, O'Grady broke away from the group and dashed down the street.

Hey! Gunnar! Robin cried. Come along, he urged Hugo, and they followed hot after their vanishing friend.

Consuelo's eyes filled with tears. Paul was petulantly angry. Campaspe's face was a mask. Vera, alone, remained entirely placid.

He's a very nice young man, Mrs. Moody remarked. I wonder why he ran away.

Seven

Two days later, a little after five o'clock in the afternoon, Campaspe again drove up to the stage-door of the Riverside Theatre. This time she made no futile attempt to besiege the gate, waiting, rather, in her car. The neighbourhood was entirely deserted at first, but presently, performers and stage-hands began to make their way out of the playhouse. It was not long, indeed, before the person whom she attended appeared, in the company of the Brothers Steel. She drew his attention with her eyes and he approached, indubitably with reluctance and even with suspicion. There was, however, Campaspe recognized, something inevitable about his appropinquation. However distasteful to him was this re-encounter, he could not, it was clear, help himself to escape it. Some power quite apart from her own desire had created this condition: of that fact, too, she was instinctively aware.

I felt an inclination for conversation, she explained lightly. Will you drive with me?

Stammering an obviously unwilling assent, he made his excuses to Robin and Hugo and entered the car.

The day was crisp and cold, with a brisk wind blowing, but the interior of the automobile was warm and comfortable. For a time the two sat silent. Campaspe did not immediately even look at her new friend. Another might have opened the conversation by remarking, You are wondering why I asked you to come, but Campaspe did nothing of the sort. Instead, she demanded abruptly, as if she had sought him out only to learn the answer, What do you think of Consuelo?

Consuelo? He seemed bewildered, and yet relieved.

The child you met in the flower-shop.

O, the child! I've thought a good deal about her. She interested me. The Persians have a proverb: A tree which comes quickly to maturity never grows very high. He spoke with difficulty. An unwonted embarrassment clouded his tone and gave his phrases a stilted air. He enunciated with great precision, although his intonation was more foreign than usual, with almost a trace of an accent. The car was driving down Riverside Drive. Campaspe ostensibly interested herself with a view of the river.

After a pause Gunnar went on uneasily, as if driven by some invisible pressure to pursue this subject, Is it her father and mother? I mean, have they pushed her?

On the contrary. Her mother is horrified, her father, quiescent, amused. She seems to belong to a different race.

She is so intense. Gunnar appeared to be a little more at his ease. She lives so hard in mind and spirit. Will she burn out?

I, too, have asked myself that question, Campaspe replied soberly, but only a prophet could answer it.

A prophet! Gunnar grasped the word, as though startled by a new idea. How can one go about becoming a prophet?

Campaspe turned her eyes casually towards his face as she responded, It is the easiest and the most difficult state of being in the world to achieve. All it requires is an unceasing reliance on one's own instincts. If you become strong enough to create this magic current, in time it becomes quite possible to understand other people even when they don't understand themselves. But, she sighed, looking back across the river, how few there are who possess the essential forces of purpose and character to bring about this condition.

I know very well now what you mean, Gunnar said, and I think you must be a wise woman.

Some days I wonder if I am; Campaspe apparently was musing aloud. There are hours when I feel that a philosophy of life is unsupportable, that the only people who really live are those who blunder and stumble blindly through.

No, not that! the young man cried vehemently. Never that! His face was aflame with a passionate denial.

What then? she demanded quickly, as if his contradictory spirit had amazed her.

He became calmer at once. I only mean to say, he explained coldly, that the plan, or lack of plan, you have just suggested is not my ideal.

She did not ask him to define his ideal. Instead, she lighted a cigarette, and inquired, Have you seen Paul?

Yes. He came to our gymnasium again last night. Paul has made a great decision: he is going to work.

But are you so sure, was Campaspe's next question, that work will be good for Paul?

Of course, I am. Work is good for everybody. It is even necessary. In a way, he continued, proudly, I made him do it.

Campaspe disregarded this boast. What about the philosopher in his ivory tower, the monk in the desert, the astronomer gazing at the stars? she catechized him.

Dust and ashes, he pronounced solemnly. They don't get anywhere. How can they? Man must work to forget the horror of infinity. These monks and philosophers prompt us to remember it.

Who does *get* anywhere? she persisted, now scrutinizing his face closely. At this moment she had a curious impression of an unterrestrial radiance glowing on his features, not unlike the flickering effulgence created by a halo.

So few, he responded sadly. Perhaps no one. I wonder if many actually try?

What, after all, does getting somewhere mean?

A new and lighter shade of feeling coloured his tone. Every one, I suppose, has his own peculiar ambitions, he averred; some desire happiness, others hanker after gold, some seek God, others, knowledge. There are those, even, who only want to forget. It seems to have occurred to no one, not even Jesus Christ or Napoleon, to aspire towards everything.

Campaspe regarded the youth with a new interest, and again she was struck by the illusion that an amber glow illumined his features. Was it, she wondered, an effect caused by the mounting of his blood under the rays of the lamp? At any rate, she believed she had never before seen such great beauty in a face, physical, spiritual, and mental beauty, and yet she observed something else there, too, dimming the glory, a suggestion of hideous pain and incessant struggle. She had made no comment after his last statement and, after a pause, he began again, Paul has at least taken a step. Before that he was only one thing, now he is on his way to many.

But I am not so sure, Campaspe argued, that many things will be good for Paul. He had his entity; he was what he was, laughing and careless, perhaps. . .

He has not showed that side of himself to me, Gunnar protested, with a trace of dismay in his tone. Not yet, Campaspe reflected, had the young man removed his eyes from Ambrose's back. If he would only look at her!

Well, he was. . . laughing and careless, until. . . she hesitated. To be perfectly frank, I noticed a certain change in Paul even before he met you.

You see. . . Gunnar was triumphant. . . he was searching.

I am not convinced that Paul has the right to search. However unconsciously, he had realized himself very neatly, very completely, I thought. I still think so. It may not have been a very big self, or a very important self, but it was Paulet's *own*.

But don't you believe in growth, in change, in accumulation, in collection? Gunnar cried out in astonishment.

I believe, Campaspe asseverated as devoutly as though she were reciting another Credo, that we are born what we are, some one way, some another, that we cannot change, no matter how hard we strive to. All we can do, with whatever amount of effort, is to drag an unsuspected quality out of its hiding place in the unconscious. If it is there, in *us,* it can neither be virtue nor vice. It can only be ourselves. Whatever it is, if we admit that it belongs to us, we need it to complete ourselves.

No! No! Gunnar cried in torment. I won't believe that! The shadow of torture fell athwart his countenance. Do you think we can get no help from outside?

Yes, that is what I think, that is what I *know,* that we can hope for no help from outside. . . unless, she qualified this statement, perhaps there may be those who utilize the people they encounter as mirrors. There are times, she went on, when I watch another act, or hear another speak, when I feel at once that this is some hitherto unsuspected part of myself that I have forgotten, or possibly never known about before at all.

Gunnar was making an effort to pull himself together. As she watched him erase the shadow from his face, quickly her mind reverted to Magdalen Roberts and her pamphlet on The Importance of the Façade. At last, he spoke: Well, possibly the desire to work is a part of Paul that he has forgotten or else never known about.

Campaspe smiled. I doubt that, she said.

If I could believe what you say, Gunnar went on in a kind of reverie, I think it might satisfy me to be like every one else.

But my belief depends on the premise that each of us is a different individual.

Each of us is God, Gunnar asserted with determination. Each can be what he desires to make himself.

Once again Campaspe forfeited an opportunity for asking the obvious question. She appeared to be meditating. And those philosophers in their ivory towers, those desert monks, those astronomers, she insisted, are they not striving to make themselves what they want to be?

It is not enough, Gunnar averred simply. Nothing is enough.

And what is the end of the quest?

There is no end to the quest. There never can be.

Campaspe went back. I fear, she remarked, that Paul has embarked on a ship which has no destination in view. How much happier he might be had he remained safely at home.

Happier, quite possibly. Worthier, no.

I doubt if Paul were created to be a worthy person.

It is his step.

It is your example.

It is, he maintained, a little complacently, Campaspe thought, a good one.

Should I, too, follow it?

That depends entirely on your inclination.

I am interested in your ideas.

You do not know what they are. There was a touch of tragic brusqueness in this retort.

Why did you come for me today? Gunnar demanded abruptly.

Why did you come with me? Campaspe countered.

Perhaps I wanted to find out why you had asked me. Perhaps. . . He hesitated. His confusion was apparent:

Her tone shifted. She adopted her most charming manner.

I came for you, she said, because I felt certain that I should be interested in a man who had enthralled both Paulet and Consuelo, in a man whose occupation seems to hover between manual and clerical labour and professional gymnastics. I have not been disappointed, she concluded.

Gunnar groaned. I have walked so far, so light-heartedly, so proudly, so easily, he mumbled. Then, with a sudden transition, Please ask your man to stop the car. His eyelashes were wet.

Let me take you home.

Please ask him to stop.

She did not try again to persuade him. She gave Ambrose the order. As the automobile drew up at the kerb and Gunnar prepared to alight, she took his hand. When, she asked, will you come to see me?

Averting his gaze, he stammered, I am working so hard now. . . Good God! . . . Lunging out of the car, he disappeared almost immediately in the dusk of distance. Campaspe peered through the window, but the only spectacle that rewarded her gaze was the Hotel Shelton, climbing in fragile grace towards the sky.

FREDERIKA HAD BUILT UP THE dying fire. Resting one foot on the fender, her legs crossed, Campaspe cupped her chin in her palm, while she considered the curious veils which hang between two personalities. She sensed a definite impression that something distasteful had occurred. A fantastic young man had approached her too closely, not quite closely enough. Riotous and chaotic, her emotions mingled with her thoughts. She was uncomfortably aware of an unpleasant transmutation. She had never before, she was beginning to believe, felt just like this. Sapiently conscious, always, of men's capacity for making fools of themselves, it had never previously been her ambition to curb this propensity. It was more satisfying, generally speaking, to examine the victim while he squirmed on the pin of her observation. Gunnar, indubitably, had aroused in her a new kind of interest. She defined this, not too literally, as an adumbration of the warm glow of motherhood. The boy was, it was apparent, too sensitive to brave the rigours of existence. The pathos of ideals! The unlocked gates of the soul! How much safer, how much more secure one felt if one understood and controlled the cells of this unlocated territory. Life based on disenchantment was comparatively sane; life based on ideals, actually dangerous. She reflected: Could she bring this young man to his senses, effect a salutary disillusion, create a realistic flower-pot in which his obviously fine qualities might blossom? Even as she considered the possibility of this ostensibly altruistic move, she was watching herself at the same time with some cynical amusement, wondering just how far she might become implicated in this drama of sympathy without breaking down her own defences, defences which, up to the present, had served her in every emergency. They had consisted in the raising of several essential bars between herself and those who came into social contact with her. She had, through this method, achieved comparative security. It had saved her the pain of doubt. She had, through its offices, enjoyed her life and she had permitted others to enjoy theirs in their fashion. She had constructed her career from the stones of disillusion: they made a strong fortress. Was she, urged by an inexplicable feeling of tenderness, lowering a drawbridge over the deep moat which separated her from the plain of suffering. Was she. . . ?

Campaspe turned to the table by her side and lifted a small volume. The world of T. F. Powys's peasants, low, mean, despicable, mechanical, material, tawdry, inflamed with hatred and greed and lust, over which hovered a nebulous power that might conceivably save, and yet always withheld a saving hand, had hitherto been sufficiently expressive to her of the world in general. She opened the leaves of The Soliloquies of a Hermit. Several passages were marked: Love one another an impossible ideal. . . people that claw and tear at each other. They steal the moods of God. They do not permit the moods of God to pour freely through them and go. . . Man is a collection of atoms through which pass the moods of God—a terrible clay picture, tragic, frail, drunken, but always deep rooted in the earth, always with claws holding on to his life while the moods pass over him and change his face and his life every moment. . . To have the soul and teeth of a lion and the body of a tramp, is the way to tread on this world as it ought to be trodden on. . . There is something very ugly about the immortal part of a man—his greed, his getting on, his self-sacrifice, his giving to the poor. I suppose there can be nothing beautiful in anything that has gone on a long while without changing; it is only the ugly part of us that can live through so many centuries of flesh and blood. . . Only at times under His yoke I have been allowed to take a little nectar from the flowers; I have hidden my hand in a waterfall of brown hair; I have caught a hurried kiss from a breathing sunbeam. This is all we can have—all. It is impossible to get more out of the world than it can give. It is best to ruminate like a cow. . . That is the way of the world, and it happens like that because man's mind can only go to a certain point, and then it breaks. Every mind breaks when it does more than a man can do, and it breaks in unexpected ways. The duty of a philosopher (and the modern philosopher knows his duty) is to keep the sheep; that is to say, to drive the wolves of thought away from the people, and hang the wolves up—in hard and long words, in the philosophers' complex minds that are fitted out with little hooks to hang each wolf up by. . . I believe that the more dead anything is the more it lasts; and the more ignoble a thing is the longer it lasts. The most base thing in me longs the most to live for ever. . . Campaspe closed the book and stared a long time into the fire. Another quotation had invaded her mind:

Voluptuousness: to the rabble the slow fire at which it is burnt: to all wormy wood, to all stinking rags, the prepared heat and stew furnace.

Voluptuousness: to free hearts, a thing innocent and free, the garden-happiness of the earth, all the future's thanks-overflow to the present.

Voluptuousness: only to the withered a sweet poison: to the lion-willed, however, the great cordial, and the reverently saved wine of wines.

Voluptuousness. . .

Eight

To his amazement Paul discovered that his Wall Street experiment was providing him with more amusement than any recognized form of diversion he had ever practised. In the course of his rounds, ambling from office to office, from bank to bank, he encountered familiar faces everywhere. He was greeted with a hearty Hello, Paul! almost as frequently as he would have been at the country club or on an opening night at the Follies. He had previously formed no conception of the vast number of men of his acquaintance who laboured in the city. Through recent observation of these old friends under conditions new to him, he was beginning to understand why so many pretty, young women who were married to elderly men found it agreeable to occupy themselves with interior decorating or to assume positions as clerks in bookshops. In business, apparently, one met all the people one knew without the disadvantages inherent in the home. Between commercial transactions, vividly exciting in themselves, one listened to all the gossip of the town. Most of these boys were well provided with Orkney, Booth's, and Bacardi. Late in the afternoon, the cocktail shaker tinkled as incessantly as it did in any uptown drawing-room. Cigars were plentiful and a profusion of varieties of expensive cigarettes inhabited boxes on every desk. Paul particularly enjoyed the interminably prolonged luncheons at the Moloch Club, quartered in luxuriously furnished rooms directly under the roof of one of the tallest sky-scrapers where, after devouring a female lobster, one might sit about for an idle hour, with Vanity Fair in one's lap, bending a careless ear to the fellow sitting next to you on the deep, comfortable couch, upholstered in brown leather, and discovering, quite casually, all the details surrounding the latest spouse-breach.

It was not so much, Paul was beginning, justifiably, to believe, to support extravagant wives that men toiled in the city, as was the opinion generally expressed, especially by foreign visitors, as it was to escape from these wives. All his life Paul had listened to business men, in the cloak-rooms at evening parties, or before the sideboard, cocktail glass in hand, or at table, after dinner, bemoan their desperate lot, threatening to retire as soon as they had succeeded in amassing a sufficiently substantial roll. Reflection engendered by his recent personal experience reminded him that he had never known one of these men to carry out this blustering plan. Nevertheless, they continued to reiterate this story to the effect that they were jumping like hell for the dollar today, but that tomorrow they proposed to quit so that they might spend the remainder of their days chasing pleasure around Europe with the Mrs.

This routine, but unpractised, philosophy, Paul soon discovered, was reserved exclusively for uptown dispensation. Observation of these fellows in their proper milieu gave him an entirely new impression of them which, quite reasonably, he conceived to be the true picture. They were having, he was by way of informing himself, an extraordinarily good time. To be sure, they dashed nimbly after the dollar, but even that part of the game resembled gambling or fox-hunting. It was an adventure replete with thrills, false trails, happy discoveries, comic coincidences. There was so much, indeed, of sportsman's luck in everything that went on there that Wall Street was prone to impress him as a kind of glorified Monte Carlo, the Circassian walnut cabinets in each office, stored with liquors and tobacco, supplying the place of the bar, while the Stock Exchange made an excellent substitute for the salle de jeu.

His spirits, accordingly, had risen appreciably, and he even found it possible to enjoy a dinner at home alone with Vera, when it was his present custom to refer portentously, after the best manner of his confrères, to his hard day in the city, and to brag of the transaction he had contrived to carry through by resorting to a vast amount of bluff, while his wife sat by, humbly esteeming this industrial brilliancy on the part of her Viking-like husband.

One day in the club, Paul encountered John Armstrong, who laid a strong arm across his shoulders as he saluted him with a Well, old fellow, what are you doing here?

I'm with Lorillard and Company, Paul explained.

The hell you are! How's Mrs. Lorillard? I haven't run into her in years.

'Paspe's just the same.

A cold woman! I never understood her. Inconceivable as it might seem, John Armstrong appeared to be brooding. I don't think I've seen her, he went on, after a pause, since the night we all went to Coney Island.

And picked up Zimbule.

That's the night! Say, she's *somebody* now! Well, he continued, I've been married since then. Got a kid.

That's quick work. I think I heard something about it.

Yep. Husband and father now. We live out at Great Neck. No good to keep a wife too near town. She wants to lunch with you if she's close enough. After my hard day's work I drive out, get home in time to see the kid before he goes to bed. Say, it's great! Come out with me some day.

I'd like to, John.

Whenever you want to. Just drop around to the office about four any day. We'll have a little drink and then I'll drive you out with me. John Armstrong sought a card which he passed over to Paul. Then he changed the subject: Say, do you know the ropes?

What ropes, John?

Well, for examp, the bars. Two floors up and knock three times and there's a drink for you. . . after you've been introduced.

Two floors up where?

Any damned building below Chambers Street. Say, I'll put you wise to something else, Armstrong added darkly. Look out for stenographers.

Do they belong to the Ku Klux? Paul demanded, smiling.

Worse. The cuties sit on your lap and invite you by their willing manner to take them out to dinner, and first thing you know along comes a shyster lawyer with a breach of promise blackmailing prospectus.

Whew! Paul exclaimed, not incredulous.

Sure. Cupid's been stung several times.

His name never gets into the papers.

Sure it doesn't, John Armstrong explained with some disgust. He fixes it up. Last time cost him thirty-five thous. Say, it would have paid him to stick to moving-picture stars. Zimbule O'Grady let him off easy. He's a heel when it comes to skirts. I never get caught myself, but then, he added, the Janes are crazy about me. Nuts, he emphasized, plain nuts over your Uncle John.

Then there was the other type of conversation, equally fascinating to Paul, which ran something like this:

Castor-oil's sixty-seven: watch out for a slump.

I'm getting out.

Well, I'm glad you told me. I was going to unload sooner or later, but if you're getting out that'll overload the market more'n the traffic can bear. I'll get out today myself.

That's my advice to you.

George Everest had been extremely valuable to Paul in the manipulation of certain transactions, Florizel Hammond was a mine of indelicate gossip, and Jack Draycott was always ready to take or dispense a drink. It was even amusing to lunch with Harvey Wetmore, who always asked the waiter if one order would be enough for two, as was the custom with men as rich as Harvey Wetmore. That was why, Paul reflected, they were rich.

Paul found enchantment in this delightful novelty. The rules for playing the game differed in every respect from the rules which governed uptown life, and it was part of the fun to acquire a knowledge of these. Paul wondered, indeed, why he had not experimented with the business world sooner. Far from the worst feature of this career was the fact that it seemed to be comparatively easy to make money. When you made any at all, Paul noted, you made more than he had ever been able to extract from his father at one time. Occasionally, of course, some poor chap lost his shirt, but usually a good gamble on the market, played with a tip from Cupid or George, would bring it back to him in no time. With Cupid as guardian, indeed, Paul believed he stood no chance of losing at all. He began to have dreams, as a matter of fact, of an independent income.

Cupid, he demanded one day, why the hell didn't you tell me long ago how damned attractive it was down here?

They were sitting in Mr. Lorillard's private office, panelled to the ceiling with Circassian walnut, richly grained and polished, their chairs and the desks, of the same wood, standing on a blue and yellow Chinese rug. The windows, opening between copper-coloured hangings, overlooked—the room was on the thirty-ninth floor—streets lying low in vast canyons formed by rows of towering sky-scrapers. The view included the bridge, gracefully swung on its cables across the East River, which was alive with tugs and barges. On a roof nearby, a lad with a long pole stirred a flock of pigeons to flight.

Cupid, bald and podgy, whose countenance never seemed to lose a pitiful expression of anxiety, was obviously puzzled. It's all right here, of course, he replied, but just what do you mean?

Why, the game's great, the view's immense, and it's all so damned much fun.

I suppose it is, Cupid admitted lugubriously, and yet I never enjoy it very much. Nothing ever seems to go right with me.

Bosh, old chap. Campaspe had often informed Paul that Cupid was pathetic, but somehow he had never sensed this quality in Mr. Lorillard before today. After all, one so seldom saw him on Nineteenth Street.

There's Campaspe, for instance, Cupid continued in his plaintive strain. I don't understand her and I never shall. You wouldn't either, he asserted, flushed and defiant, if you were married to her.

I understand Vera to the last eyelash. Paul grinned sardonically.

Well, there's a difference. You're not in love with Vera. I've always been wild about my wife and she treats me like. . . like. . . Cupid hesitated for a figure.

Like the father of your sons, Paul suggested.

Well, I don't know that she even does that, Cupid dubiously dissented. Then there was Zimbule, he went on, and Susan and Emily and Armide. . .

Armide?

Yes, it was her name that got me, too. She was French.

Did she burn the palace and escape on a hippogryph? Paul demanded.

I'm not sure about the hippogryph, but she certainly burned the palace. She burned it last week. The little man sighed.

I heard something about it, Paul responded sympathetically, but I didn't catch her name.

Paul, Cupid groaned, I'm a boob with women, a simp. They can get anything out of me, and the only way I can find love is to buy it. Nobody cares for me for myself.

You're a good egg, Paul assured him.

You bet your life I'm a good egg, good and easy enough to eat! Do you know what the trouble is, Paul? I should never have gone into business. I used to play the bass-viol, and if I had kept up my music I would have led an entirely different life. . . got something out of it.

Paul lighted a cigarette. What about those stocks, Cupid? he inquired.

Cupid gave him a quick, intense glance. I can't understand you, Paul. This interest of yours in affairs. You always come back to stocks. God! You're exploding a proverb! Lucky in business and lucky with women, too.

I suppose it's because I know their place, Paul explained modestly.

Don't you ever fall for a skirt? Cupid queried, wide-eyed. Doesn't it *ever* get you?

Paul reflected. I've fallen once or twice, he responded, but I guess it wasn't for a skirt. More likely, it was for a mesh-bag.

That night in the great dining-room, facing the vast wall-painting by Rubens, representing Helena Fourment in the foreground as the central figure of a Sabine rape, Paul sat at table with Vera.

I didn't like it one bit at first, that lady admitted, the dimples in her round cheeks deepening under her smiles, but now I'm proud of you, Paul.

Proud?

Yes, dear. I hate your being away all day, but I console myself by remembering that you used to go out just as much before you went to work. And now, after all, I know where you are, with all those big, strong, manly men down in Wall Street, fighting the fight for bread. Why, Mr. Whittaker was as poor as anything when he started out.

It always amused Paul to hear more about Mr. Whittaker; he took up the subject.

Did he fight hard, Vera?

Did he? She served herself to a bountiful helping of a particularly fattening variety of pudding. *Did* he? Well, he just fought until he conquered down among the bears and oxen. It was wheat that made his fortune, she mused. Ceres, the great nature goddess, did that for us. I always told Bristol that we should worship nature! Now if I had been a Roman. . . ! Her imagination was not equal to rounding out this sentence and a spoonful of pudding which she had just inserted in her mouth would have rendered the feat difficult in any case.

Wheat? Paul purred interrogatively.

O, I don't mean he mowed, Vera explained, but he took off his coat in the pit. . . and did—she waved a chubby arm as if an understanding of such matters was beyond the scope of a young and pretty woman—what men do, she concluded limpingly.

And where, she demanded, would I be if it hadn't been for Bristol fiercely tramping up and down in the pit with his coat off? Where would you be, for that matter? We're enjoying the fruits of his struggles, and Paul—her husband noted that she had assumed her most endearing manner, the manner he most feared—at first I didn't see why we shouldn't, and that's why I cried so hard when you went down there too. O! I said to myself, isn't it enough that one man has done it? Isn't one martyr enough for one cause? Why has my beloved Paul got to go down and suffer and sweat and take off his coat and die when Mr. Whittaker has already done it and left us enough to feed an army with? I thought it would be just dreadful to have you away too, Paul, until the other day I remembered that you're away so much anyway, with your friends, that it is an actual relief to know approximately where you are, and you've done so splendidly now, and it gives me so much to talk about when I go out. Paul, she concluded, offering him the glance of an amorous and dying swan, I tell everybody that *you* are supporting *me* now!

It must surprise them.

It petrifies them. And Paul, I hope you won't mind. . . but I bought this ring today. She exhibited an emerald, cut en cabochon, the size of a wren's egg.

Vera dear, why should I mind? So long as Mr. Whittaker's gold, won in the sweat and turmoil of the pit, holds out, I don't see any reason why you shouldn't buy anything you like.

O, but Paul, I haven't told you everything. I explain that *you* gave it to me!

After dinner they sat in the spacious drawing-room with its guilloches carved by Grinling Gibbons, which had been purchased by the late Mr. Whittaker from an impecunious English peer, with its massive Dutch marquetry cabinets, on which were ranged pots of splendid flowering plants, created by patient Chinese artists out of jade, alabaster, jacinth, sardonyx, beryl, agate, crystal, and cornelian. In needle-point arm-chairs husband and wife faced each other in front of the fire. Silence had fallen between them. Vera yawned occasionally; Paul, frequently.

I'm going out, Paul announced a little later.

On this awful night! Vera reproached him. It's damp and chilly and there's a nasty drizzle. I'm so afraid you'll catch cold. Where are you going? she questioned him suspiciously.

To see Gunnar.

That acrobat! I don't want to seem fussy about your friends, Paul, only you've known some strange people in your old bohemian days—I'll never forget that ridiculous Bunny—and now that you're in business I had hoped. . .

Paul rose, stretching himself, and yawned again.

Still—she was consoling herself aloud for the ineffectuality of her remonstrance—Campaspe knows him. There must be *something.*

There is, Vera, I assure you, there is something. Bending over her chair he lightly brushed the back of her head with his lips. When he had departed, the tears coursed slowly down the lonely woman's chubby cheeks. Mr. Whittaker, stern, unyielding in the matter of his prejudices, with a firmly fixed idea that a wife's place was in her home, had ruled her with his strong will, and now Paul Moody was able, she had discovered, to rule her by his very nonchalance. Well, she reflected, to salve the pain of the knowledge, men must work and women must weep.

Paul did not call the car from the garage, nor did he hail a taxi. He had donned a heavy, waterproof coat and, without the protection of an umbrella, he strode with long paces through the rain-swept streets. The beating of the stinging drops against his cheeks invigorated and refreshed him. His customary cheerful spirit returned. Life was amusing, after all. Work was amusing. Even Vera contributed her share to the savour of his happiness. She made so little trouble and she possessed such a delightfully unconscious vein of humour. As Paul stepped into a doorway to light a cigarette, he began to chuckle over a new idea which had occurred to him. How ironic, how ludicrously perverse, it would be to support Vera, supposing war or failure or some other great human or natural force should suddenly sweep away the Whittaker millions!

With such idle reflections he whiled away his walk until, almost before he was aware of it, he was climbing the stairs which led to the atelier of the Brothers Steel. In response to his knock Mrs. Hugo opened the door.

O, Mr. Moody, she cried, I'm so glad to see you!

Where are the boys?

Why, they're not home from the show yet. I was just cookin' supper for them.

Paul consulted his watch. It's just after ten, he said. How long. . . ?

Any minute, now. They got a better spot on the bill this week. They're Number 1.

Where are they working?

Brooklyn. Of course, she went on, with a courageous interpretation of the facts of life, the while she stirred a mixture in the pot on the stove with a long spoon, Number 1 isn't the *best* spot, but it's better to have folks walkin' in on you than walkin' out on you.

In the circumstances Paul considered this excellent philosophy; under other conditions he wondered if it would be as true.

At this juncture, the knob turned slowly in the door and the brothers, muffled in scarfs and greatcoats, entered. Their manner was gloomy and solemn, and they were unaccompanied.

Hello, mother. Hello, Paul, they glumly muttered in unison.

Why, what's the matter? Mrs. Hugo dropped her spoon.

Just as bad as can be, said Robin.

Worse, Hugo moaned.

Their jaws dropped.

Well now, is your time cancelled?

Worse, Hugo jerked out.

You didn't sprain your wrist again? She felt the pulse of her physically sound husband.

Worse, Robin groaned, much, much worse.

Gunnar's left us, mother, Hugo was at last able to explain.

Gone! Robin sobbed.

The twins had seated themselves side by side on the bench against the wall, their huge shoulders meeting, the pattern of their moustaches repeating itself ridiculously on their dejected countenances.

Nine

The disappearance of Gunnar, on the whole, aroused comparatively little astonishment in Campaspe; she was not, however, altogether free from a certain sensation of relief. There had been, she was fully aware, underground rumblings in their latest conversation which foretold in hollow tones the advent of emotional earthquakings. To tread lightheartedly over such fissures, portents of the anger of nature, had not been, hitherto, too difficult for a lady who protected herself with an adroitly secure philosophy, a philosophy which, supported by a few simple rules in respect to conduct, had never yet failed her even when the way split, figuratively speaking, under her feet. In this instance, however, she foresaw that the fissures would open between her and another, whose guiding star of idealism might not lead him safely to stable ground. He might conceivably, she argued, with a part of herself that seldom became conscious, appeal to her for aid in this extra-emergency, and push or pull her with him into the aching jaws of the chasm. He had had, she assured herself, a like premonition of impending disaster, and had rescued himself by the obvious device of running away from the danger, a habitual propensity of his, she noted, not without annoyance. Campaspe's own temperament forbad her to run away from anything. She was prepared to face whatever came towards her; in most instances, indeed, to welcome it; more, to beckon it excitedly. She had, as a matter of fact, up to this moment, taken the initiative in the precise drama undergoing her present consideration, and so it was with a curious foreboding that she experienced, quite uncharacteristically, this vast sensation of relief in the knowledge of Gunnar's flight, combined with the feeling that his action had preserved her, at least momentarily, from an unknown peril of which she was just a little afraid. Nevertheless, with this sensation of relief came to her simultaneously a glimmering of regret, for there was that unique perversity in her emotional make-up which made her grieve for nothing quite so poignantly as for discarded experience. It was Gunnar, however, who had created the vacuum, if there were a vacuum—sometimes, pondering in an obscure and contradictory reverie, it was given to her to doubt even this—a thought which afforded her sufficient consolation so that, along with whatever other loss she had suffered, she suffered no concomitant loss of self-respect.

Meanwhile the rapidly unwinding panorama of New York life continued to display itself before her somewhat listless perceptions. A tenet of her serviceable philosophy informed her that, if the complete satisfying of any desire were for some reason impossible there was always a substitute, a theory which, if it did not appear to hold as much plausibility as formerly, was at any rate still sufficiently reassuring to encourage her to look about, and, as always, she found something to look at. Laura, trembling before the precocity of Consuelo, in turn applauded by George, was a complex spectacle that would have commanded her attention to the exclusion of all other exhibitions in a more propitious period. Even in her present mood this show succeeded in arousing a good deal of her latent interest. Further, the extraordinary case of Paul offered her abundant material for cogitation. Paul, invading Cupid's realm, apparently a slave to the hitherto unsuspected delights of the marts of trade and commerce, served to excellently substantiate her conviction that it was never advisable to decline to drink out of any fountain before one had sampled the water. Vera, too, unhappy Vera, plunged alternately into depths of liquid melancholy and unpleasant and ungovernable demonstrations of blustering fatuousness by this metamorphosis in the supposedly natural characteristics of her spouse, was another object to repay at least superficial study.

Musing in such a manner one day, Campaspe began to believe that enough blessings in the way of vicarious emotion had been vouchsafed her so that she might devote a few idle moments to the casual inspection of a book with an unpromising title. Upon examination, this unlikely volume rewarded her none too close scrutiny with novel information concerning certain architectural aberrations in the world with which she had been, until then, entirely unfamiliar. It was delightful, for example, to read about the insane but realized structural fantasy known as the Villa Palagonia. The eccentric Prince who had caused the erection of this edifice had filled his courtyard with statues of unseemly monsters, of which, it appeared, he lived in some fear. Another of his idiosyncrasies was the collection of the horns and antlers of every known mammal that carried these utilitarian decorations. He also indulged a frantic passion for mirrors. His ballroom was roofed and walled with looking-glasses. Further, it had been the Prince's fancy to construct his dining-room in the form of a horse-shoe, a symbol repeated in the shape of the table. The walls of this chamber were inlaid with Chinese porcelain, giving the place the appearance of a huge vase, while the furniture was inlaid with mirrors.

Nor was it disagreeable to peruse the account of the Palace-Convent of Mafra, erected near Lisbon by King João V, in an attempt, more or less successful, to rival the gloomy splendour of the Escurial. The chambers of this building were of such mammoth proportions that the walls could scarcely be counted on interminably to support the heavy ceilings, but these walls were so cunningly constructed that if they fell they would fall inward, burying under the weight of stones the secret of the creation of this palace, if there were a secret. Again, it was diverting to become acquainted with the baroque harmonies of the Prefettura and Seminario, reared in a stone of a golden hue, so soft when quarried that it might be carved into the most fantastic shapes before, in a few days, it hardened, in the Apulian town of Lecce which, she noted with a smile, was famous for the manufacture of that essential eighteenth century commodity, castrati, an industry as much frowned on legally in that epoch as bootlegging is today. There was always, Campaspe still believed, something left to think about.

Moreover, as the day wore on, other distractions presented themselves so that, as yet, there seemed to be no occasion for her to apply to Swamis, Coués, or Freuds. She recognized the fact, however, that the world in general, and New York in particular, would lose a great deal of their savour if there were not some persons who continued to subscribe to the panaceas advocated by these hierophants, performing all the prescribed rites with due solemnity. They were an essential part of the human circus and she knew that she would miss them if they were absent. Nevertheless, what she craved most in her present mood was a certain wholesome sanity, and where could she ever hope to find that again? Was there, she wondered, no shadow of it left on this sphere save that by no means modest share which she locked in her own bosom?

The distractions were various. A cabinet-maker arrived for the purpose of restoring a Boulle desk of which a great deal of the brass scroll-work was missing, but, after an interview with him, Campaspe decided to leave the wreck, for the time being, in its present condition. The artisan was so little conversant with the properties of this type of furniture that he had even referred to the tortoise-shell as lacquer. A little later, she tried some Chinese records, which had just been sent to her, on the phonograph, and was amazed to discover how clear and pellucid, how limpidly lovely, this music was. It was the kind of music, indeed, that the more sophisticated French and Spanish composers were just beginning to compose, and Chinese music had always been referred to as ugly noises! I might have known, she averred to herself, that a race which has understood every other art for centuries would not be backward in the art of music. And she marvelled that it had been possible for any admirer of Mozart to disregard the magic of this oriental melody with its odd rhythms, its rigidly irregular monotony, and its fascinating clang-tints. From Chinese music her thoughts escaped to a consideration of the curiously sure genius of a young Mexican boy, Miguel Covarrubias, who created caricatures of celebrities, whom he knew only by sight and name, which exposed the whole secret of the subjects' personalities. Here was clairvoyance. And his drawings of Negroes crystalized the essential characteristics of the race, withal each was drawn with as eager an eye for individual traits as directed the pen of Albrecht Dürer. Material for admiration here. This meditation was interrupted by a summons from the cook.

Now ordinarily—indeed, invariably—the cook was Frederika's job. Frederika engaged the cook, ordered the meals, and when she was unsatisfactory, discharged her. Campaspe could not recall that she had ever seen this particular cook, so that it was not without a certain amount of curiosity that she received Frederika's breathless announcement that this servant demanded an audience. She insists on complaining to you personally, Frederika apologized, and says she'll go if you won't see her. She's a very good cook, the maid added, in palliation for this unusual procedure of the unloading of her own troubles on Campaspe's back. Campaspe decided at once that she would humour the woman, but she spent a few moments amusing herself by selecting the setting for the interview. Should she invade the kitchen or should she invite the cook to confer with her in the drawing-room? She gave her ultimate approval to the former location and was pleased with her choice when she stood facing this great, raw-boned, gaunt and elderly, Irish female, with stray wisps of grey hair and red face with promnent cheek-bones, lustily stirring a mixture in a brown crockery bowl on the table before her. She did not desist when confronted by her mistress, nor did she invite her to sit down. Was it etiquette, Campaspe demanded of herself, for a cook in her own domain to request her employer to seat herself? She listened to the cook's complaint, which included a diatribe against the scullery-maid whose belief in Christian Science made her presence distasteful to the cook who was a Catholic. The waitress, it appeared, had a policeman keeping company with her, and Frederika occasionally helped herself to a nip of sherry. These denunciations were delivered in a belligerent fashion and accompanied by a prodigious stirring of the mixture in the bowl which, Campaspe realized with a sort of awe, was something she herself would be eating later in the day. The performance was concluded with a florid peroration of some length in which the cook summed up her troubles and cried, Them or me goes, standing arms akimbo, the great wooden spoon stuck out at a right angle, so that it suggested some mysterious mediæval weapon. Never previously, Campaspe assured herself, had she known so much about the private lives of her servants. It gave her the impression that she was a feudal lord dispensing justice to his serfs. Nevertheless, she recognized her impotence. She could scarcely limit the choice of the waitress in the matter of young men, nor could she instruct the scullery-maid to alter her faith. Frederika's taste for sherry, as a matter of fact, seemed highly creditable. As Solomon, Campaspe said to herself, I am a failure. I cannot render decisions. She relied, instead, on a formula which had proved efficacious in many similar situations in other ranks of life. She entreated the cook to comprehend that she was a superior person who should be able to get along with her inferiors. They know no better, these others, she explained; so let them have their way. This argument, she could see, was not without making its effect. The cook, indeed, warmed perceptibly, sufficiently, at any rate, so that she returned to her work. As an additional precaution, Campaspe suggested to Frederika the advisability of offering the cook a nip of sherry now and then. She also inquired of the waitress if she were acquainted with another policeman sufficiently blind to feminine charm so that he might be persuaded to call occasionally on the cook. Then she dismissed the matter from her mind.

The letters of the past few days had gathered on a tray and it now occurred to Campaspe that she might take the time to look these over. For the most part, as she had presurmised, they were not of any great import. The inspection of invitations and bills never succeeded in giving her much pleasure, but it was fun to open an invitation to a luncheon which had been given the day before "to meet Lady Diana Manners," and to read a typewritten epistle requesting her to serve on a committee to decide what kind of animal the Girl Scouts of America should present to the Bronx Zoo. I think, she murmured to herself, that I shall recommend a garter snake. A characteristic note from Lalla Draycott she dropped after glancing at a line or two. At the bottom of the heap, or as near the bottom as Campaspe ever penetrated, she discovered a large envelope from the Ritz, addressed in a feeble, scrawling hand, which she did not immediately recognize. On examination it proved to be from the Countess Nattatorrini who, it seemed, had arrived in New York.

Campaspe had met the Countess one afternoon several years before at the hôtel of the Duchess of Guermantes. The occasion, on the whole, had been dull enough; still, Campaspe had derived a certain oblique entertainment from listening to Oriane discuss the peculiar reasons why she could and did know certain people and the still better reasons why she could not know others. Presently, the Countess, who even then must have been in her seventies, had gravitated towards her, believing her doubtless to be a person of some importance, as she was the only American, with the exception of her titled self, she had ever known Oriane to invite to her house. The curious confusion of grande dame and courtesan which Campaspe had at once sensed in the countenance of this elderly lady had caused her to make an effort to create a sympathetic atmosphere, which had proved sufficiently alluring so that the Countess had asked her to lunch with her the next day, and then and there began a friendship based, on the part of the Countess, on a blind desire to discover an indulgent listener, and, on Campaspe's part, on a willingness to listen. Then one day, the confessional had become a shambles. Throwing off what little remained of her reserve, the Countess had related the sorry details of her curiously monotonous career, like casting swine before pearls, Campaspe thought, and she wondered if she had been the Countess's only confessor save the priest, so complete was the woman's self-denigration and so passionate her enjoyment of it. Their relationship had assumed more formality after this breach in decorum—it is natural to turn against a person to whom you have told too much about yourself—and soon after Campaspe had left Paris. Since then, whenever she had visited the French capital, the Countess had been away en villégiature or in London, so that this was the first opportunity offered her to renew the acquaintanceship. Noting that the letter had been mailed two days earlier, she sent Frederika at once to the telephone with instructions.

In a few moments the maid returned. The Countess is not feeling very well, she explained, and does not wish to go out. She asks if you will lunch with her.

Of course, Campaspe replied. Tell her I shall be delighted.

On the way to the Ritz she recalled that she had agreed to join Hubert Miles and his young wife at Voisin's, but she did not regret this lapse of memory which, perhaps, had not been altogether unconscious. Driving up Park Avenue she peered ahead at the terraced apartment houses rising on either side. Soon, she mused, New York will resemble ancient Babylon. It will become a city of terraced palaces, with balconies and aerial gardens. How much New Yorkers like to move! There is the endless search for a new environment. The average life of any smart colony is only five years. It will soon be as bad form to live on Park Avenue as it is now to live on Riverside Drive. The present pilgrimage is towards the East River around Sutton Place or Beekman Place. In ten years, First Avenue, which adjoins these localities, will probably be the Park Avenue of its decade. Then Campaspe's mind reverted to a street further up the river she had herself discovered, a delightfully quiet street facing a little park. Later, in the spring, the boats on the stream could be discerned through the green of the trees. No one else had yet marked the charm of this particular spot. If I bought a house there I suppose enough of my world would follow me to make it a profitable investment, Campaspe reflected.

The formal Louis XVI drawing-room, in the suite occupied by the Countess, invaded by the contents of her trunks, was in appalling disorder. Robes were strewn over all the chairs, but tall crystal vases of American Beauty roses gave a sense of decorative grace to the place. Through an open doorway Campaspe caught a glimpse of three innovation trunks standing open in the bedroom. Chairs, bed, and floor were littered with a profusion of hats and gowns from the Parisian couturières, while a maid struggled futilely to put an end to this confusion.

My trunks have just arrived; I had such difficulties with the douane, the Countess explained, after kissing Campaspe on both cheeks. You will pardon the appearance of my rooms. . .

She chattered on in a kind of passionate endeavour to keep from thinking, Campaspe decided, as she made a rapid examination of the figure before her. At first, the false teeth, the hollow cheeks, artfully tinted with red, the ravaged throat, concealed beneath a broad band of black velvet, were a trifle repulsive, but in a little while, this unfortunate initial impression wore away. After all, Campaspe summed it up, she is seventy-seven; may I look as well when I attain that age! She was truly amazing, this woman. Her figure was not bad: her dress made it even presentable. Her white hair gave her an air of distinction, and Campaspe again mentally admired the contradictions in her face, her full sensual lips and staring eyes, mingled with an expression that stamped her at heart as utterly conventional. Possibly Iowa had presented her with this paradoxical respectability. However that might be, it was the quality that had saved the Countess from the gutter, Campaspe realized.

It soon became evident that Madame Nattatorrini was fortunate only in appearance. In other respects she was a pathetic, old woman, as restless as the Wandering Jew, always searching and never finding. The undiscovered secret of perpetual motion might, after all, be lust. Why had no inventor ever contrived to enslave this terrifying force, to turn it to practical account? There was not, to be sure, more than a hint of this vehement, unsatisfied desire in the actual words used by the Countess in speaking, but it was easy for Campaspe to look through the nervous, the almost shrill, commonplaces of what was said into the harassed soul of senile agony and longing.

Paris is so tiresome! the Countess was complaining, after an extended account of her prolonged argument with the customs officials. I felt I could bear it no longer. I was dying for a change! She threw out her arms and tossed her head. Would New York, I wondered, offer me what I wanted? I have heard so much about the post-war gaieties here. Some of my friends have told me that it is the most brilliant city in the world today. I wanted to try it. Shall we lunch up here? I don't feel very fit today, not well enough to face a crowd in the restaurant. Alceste, nous voulons déjeuner ici. But, she continued, without a break, it is so cold, so rainy, so forbidding. I recall that the sun used to shine in America in the winter. I think I should like to go to Buenos Ayres, to the Argentine, to get warm. I saw Valentino in that picture! What a handsome fellow he is! South America must be warmer, but there is no one to go with me.

I wish I might take the trip with you, Campaspe interjected, instantly detecting the Countess's mental rejection of any such proposal.

I should have married again; I am so much alone, the Countess sighed, while the waiter offered her the menu. Will you try the sole? I should have borne children, like you. When you reach my age you will have your babies, your own sons—Ella's expression was avid at the mention of this sex—to be with you, to go with you where you will. I am all alone. What will you eat?

That question settled, the waiter having departed to execute the order, the Countess burst forth again: He was *extremely* good-looking. There was a line to his nose. Do they have Greek waiters here? The Swiss are *so* short. . . Paris is so dull. What is every one doing here? No, I don't play Mah Jong. . . I know so few people in New York intimately—I've spent so much of my life with foreigners. Perhaps, it has been all wrong. Do you think it is too late? O, Campaspe, you must help me to undo the effect on my spirits caused by this rain! Does it rain all the time here? It's even worse than Paris.

You'll see the sun occasionally, Campaspe replied. On days like this I usually keep my curtains drawn. I never know that the weather is bad unless I go out.

I'm tired of the theatre, the Countess went on. I hear that Gareth Johns is in town. Twenty-six years ago, she sighed, it was that. . . Have you seen him? Have you met his wife?

Not yet. I expect to meet them next week.

What is his wife like? Have you heard? He married her, you know, for her money.

No, I haven't heard, but I know what she must be like. She's a quiet, little woman, rather frumpy probably, who smoothes out his moods and polishes off the rough contacts. The life of an author's wife is the life of a laundress. Always washing and ironing!

Campaspe, you are delicious. The Countess was amused for the first time, and an expression of pleasure spread over her countenance. I knew I should do well to come to New York. You will cheer me up in spite of the rain!

An hour later, as she drove away from this encounter, Campaspe felt a new twinge of her morning dissatisfaction. There was getting to be too much of this sort of thing in the world. Was there, she asked her gods, no hint of sanity anywhere?

Ten

George, Laura Everest tearfully exclaimed to her husband one evening on his return from the city, I just don't know what to do about Consuelo!

What's the trouble now, Laura? George demanded indifferently, a trifle bored by his wife's chronic, if still bewildered, complaint.

She wants to become an acrobat, wants to study with those awful circus people she met through Campaspe.

George chuckled. I thought she met them first.

Well, at any rate she never would have seen that man again if Campaspe hadn't invited her to go to the Riverside. If I had known. . . !

Why not let her, Laura?

Are you out of your head, George?

George shielded a permanent smile behind the newspaper he held in his hands as he persisted, Why not let her, I say? All the babies in town are doing something of the sort now. Hiram Mason's son is studying pugilism, doubtless with the intention of challenging Young Stribling. Ira Barber's little girl is striving to acquire the rudiments of interpretative dancing. Already her picture, in Greek costume, has appeared in the illustrated section of the Sunday Times. Maida Sonsconsett, aged nine, attends the Institute where Dalcroze Eurythmics are expounded, and Helen Blair has gone in for Gurdjieff. . .

That is an entirely different matter, and you know it, George, Laura expostulated. Everybody has gone in for Gurdjieff, but acrobats are vulgar.

Laura dear, you're not up on acrobats. Why, I recently read somewhere or other that all circus performers are good to their wives, never get divorces, and attend church services regularly. They never drink and they never swear. Laura, if the younger generation is insisting on physical training, I don't think we could put Consuelo in more moral hands.

George, you're not serious. You are praising middle-class virtues. Do you want your daughter brought up that way?

I *am* serious. I don't think it would do Consuelo any harm at all to imbibe a few middle-class ideas. Of course, we'll ask Miss Pinchon to accompany her to the studio or whatever they call it and chaperon Consuelo while she takes her lesson. In a short time, doubtless, she will be able to turn cartwheels and handsprings all over the drawing-room floor. The Masons and the Sonsconsetts and the Barbers and the Blairs will die of envy. I predict that you'll live to see an epidemic of fashionable acrobats. Think of it: they can all perform together like a troupe of Arabs. You'll always have entertainment for an evening party. And if I lose my money, he added slyly, Consuelo will have a profession. She can support us in our old age.

George! Will you never be serious?

Laura, Consuelo knows too much. George certainly was more serious now. Why, already she's read books that you and I will never read, and probably wouldn't understand if we did. This is a dangerous state of affairs. If we don't look out for her she'll fall ill. Physical culture is the very thing she needs.

She'll develop horrid muscles on her arms and legs!

You're thinking of the ballet. This sort of thing is quite different, Laura. She won't learn to stand on her toes; she'll learn to stand on her head.

Ultimately Laura was persuaded if not convinced. A day or so later, vetoing her final protestations, George paid a call on the Brothers Steel to discuss the matter. Hugo and Robin, disconsolate over the defection of Gunnar, their booking over the Orpheum Circuit cancelled and their time on the Pantages dated a month ahead, were immeasurably cheered by the profitable prospect that opened before them, and gave their ready assent to the plan.

After George Everest's departure, sitting, as was their wont, side by side on the long bench, stroking their moustaches in unison, their faces actually assumed an expression of hope. Observing this sign, Mrs. Hugo suggested that the scheme had infinite future possibilities. You'd be home all the time, boys, and I'm sure you'll get more pupils and make a pile of money, and never have to worry about bookin' no more. This was, indeed, they believed, a new idea which might prove remunerative. Now that a connection had been formed with the upper East Side, more rich little boys and girls might be induced to apply for instruction in the acrobatic arts. If this possibility faded, they might take on poor little boys and girls and train them for the circus and the vaudeville stage. The idea had never occurred to them before, and now it had been put into their heads by a business man from Wall Street! If Gunnar were only here to offer them advice and encouragement! Their faces fell again.

One morning, shortly after their interview with her father, Consuelo, accompanied by Miss Pinchon, appeared at the gymnasium. Mrs. Hugo conducted the child behind the curtains and assisted her in donning the costume which her mother had provided. When she emerged from the recess, her arms bare, her slender hips encased in baggy knickerbockers, she presented, with her pale, solemn face, shadowed by golden curls, her great staring eyes, and her slender arms and legs, an extremely curious picture. Miss Pinchon had brought a book with her, but she did not open it. Her gaze was portentously ardent.

Well, Miss Consuelo, whadya want to learn? Robin demanded politely.

I want to do everything that Gunnar can do, she replied without hesitation.

Whew! Some ambish! Hugo cried. It'll take a long time.

I expect it to, Consuelo calmly assured him, the longer the better.

When the primitive first excercises began, Consuelo in the gravest manner devoted her whole soul to the accomplishment of what was demanded of her, while Miss Pinchon studied the execution of the evolutions with an attention which seemed entirely out of proportion to the spectacle offered to her vision.

When do you expect Gunnar back? Consuelo inquired, suspending her fatiguing exercise.

The twins, who had been in the best of spirits, wilted at this question.

You mustn't ask about Gunnar, dearie, Mrs. Hugo patiently explained. We don't know when he'll be back.

If ever, Robin solemnly added.

Consuelo appeared not to have taken this in. Well, she urged, I'm rested now. Let's go back to work.

Day after day the lessons continued, Consuelo throwing all her nervous energy, all her intelligence, into the achievement of professional agility. She proved pliable and exceedingly limber. It was amazing how fast she learned. It was necessary at first, of course, to give her excercises for the strengthening of the muscles, and these she was advised to practise at home. She followed this counsel with so much assiduity that for the time being she entirely neglected her reading. Every morning, accompanied by Miss Pinchon, she visited the brothers for a lesson. The governess, seated on a hard, wooden chair, did not appear to be uncomfortable. A vague idea was gradually becoming concrete in Miss Pinchon's brain.

Consuelo's parents were by no means blind to the physical improvement in the child. Even Laura was now satisfied that some good might come out of this vagary.

If there were only a philosophy behind this, George chucklingly remarked to Campaspe one day, there would be no stopping it. All it needs is a philosophy. . . something about soul hunger being satisfied. . . and then every mother in New York would send her child down there.

I am not altogether certain, Campaspe suggested, that there is not a philosophy behind it.

Well, you know what I mean, the mystified George countered.

Yes, I know what you mean, was Campaspe's cryptic response.

While they were talking in the Everest drawing-room, Miss Pinchon crossed the room, ostensibly in search of a book. There was an expression on her face that no one had ever seen there before. No one, as a matter of fact, observed it now.

Eleven

Mrs. Humphry Pollanger—Isabel, her intimate friends called her—occupied an anomalous and at the same time a strategic position in New York society. Without much difficulty she could trace her ancestry back to Anneke Jans Bogardus and, therefore, had she been so inclined, she was entitled to ally herself with the horde of similar descendants who sporadically sued Trinity Church Corporation for recognition of their proprietary rights in the sixty-three acres in lower Manhattan, much more valuable now than they were in the middle of the seventeenth century when Mrs. Bogardus died in what was then known as New Amsterdam. Mrs. Pollanger, however, did not entertain any such inclination. She had plenty of money, plenty of blood; her amiable ambition was for brains. So she joined all the women's clubs she could discover, wrote a paper on The Relationship of the American Woman to the Young Intellectuals which, published in the Century, automatically admitted her to membership in the Authors' League, furnished her house with early American furniture, and entertained every visiting celebrity who would give her the privilege of doing so. She, therefore, constituted the bridge—practically the only effectual one since Edith Dale's Washington Square salon had been abandoned—between the professional world and what the New York Journal called "exclusive social circles." These two classes never mingle very successfully, although individuals may wander from one to the other without causing consternation. The result was that, after a short time, Mrs. Pollanger was looked upon by the authors as a woman of society, while the smart world regarded her as a club woman. Everybody laughed at her a good deal behind her back, but everybody went to her parties to eat the peerless chaud-froid, created by her French cook, and to consume the apparently inexhaustible supply of Pol Roger. Besides, these parties were amusing, although frequently unintentionally so. For one thing, the guests could count on the presence of Mr. Humphry Pollanger, who was vaguely known to sit behind a desk somewhere near Wall Street, cutting off coupons and signing papers for an hour or two each day. He attended these parties, but never seemed to be quite as much at home as his wife's friends. It frequently happened, indeed, that he was urged by some one who had not been introduced to him to take another glass of wine. He had even been mistaken, on occasion, for Mrs. Pollanger's butler.

When the newspapers announced that Gareth Johns would return to America for the first time in ten years, for the first time, that is, since his fame as a novelist had become international, his works now appearing in the Tauchnitz edition as fast as they were issued and even in Spanish and Swedish translations, it had been a foregone conclusion that Mrs. Pollanger would give some kind of entertainment for him. Her social gatherings assumed various forms; sometimes, as was the case with Hugh Walpole, she invited a few friends to a small informal dinner; sometimes, as was the case with Frank Swinnerton, she gave a large, informal breakfast. She had collected a theatre party to honour Lord Dunsany and she had arranged a ball for Rebecca West. Local celebrities, such as Joseph Hergesheimer, Sinclair Lewis, Carl Van Vechten, and Theodore Dreiser, were often bidden to attend these functions, and occasionally, if seldom, she included one or more of these in her dinner lists, but she had never been able to lure James Branch Cabell from Dumbarton, Virginia, into her house.

The house, as has been reported, was furnished in an early American style, the inappropriateness of which decorative scheme struck Campaspe more vividly than ever before, as she ascended the grand staircase with Jack and Lalla Draycott at eleven o'clock. She cherished her own peculiar ideas on the subject of period furniture, one of which was that people who lived in any epoch must always have retained in their homes chairs and tables and commodes and secretaries from preceding decades. Assuredly, no one was going to throw out Regency beds or Louis XIV tables that had belonged to one's mother because one happened to live in the time of Louis XV. Campaspe held another theory to the effect that all the comfortable furniture of any period was speedily worn out and discarded; only the ball-room chairs, the heavy, carved settles, and other like cheerless lumber, survived the hard usage of one age in sufficiently good condition to pass on to another. As time passed, even the *semi*-comfortable pieces began to decay, so that, if you were determined to furnish your house in the style of an epoch two or three centuries back you were obliged to rely on solid, stiff-backed chairs, and cupboards and beds, built, apparently, for eternity. In regard to the particular style chosen for the decoration of this particular house, possibly for patriotic reasons, for Mrs. Pollanger was loud in her praise of everything American, but more conceivably because it was fashionable at present and therefore expensive, Campaspe was repelled by its obvious incongruity. The grand piano and the modern, brightly hued dresses of the women, were assuredly ridiculous in this milieu. Perfect taste demanded that this setting should be occupied by men and women dressed in a sober, Puritan fashion, but it demanded in vain.

As Campaspe, flanked by her companions, approached the drawing-room, she drew her cloak of flamingo feathers more closely around the silver-grey of her clinging robe, and hesitated near the doorway, as she became aware that the standing group within was listening to a contralto of imposing, but finely moulded, proportions, singing La Chevelure. Her eye aimed its way across the room to where the woman stood, tall, handsome, massive, her blue-black hair, knotted in the back and bit by a coral comb, drawn severely away from her white face, slit by magenta lips. The singer, Campaspe next observed, wore a black velvet gown, short in front, but trailing behind, thickly embroidered in a design of bursting pomegranates, fashioned of seed-pearls and rose tourmalines. This, she reflected, was no time or place to sing this song, certainly not with the shameless effrontery with which this woman sang it. A mood of embarrassment, a cold reaction, beset the room.

Campaspe's eye roved, although her ear was still attentive: standing on the dais near the performer, she saw Isabel Pollanger, elaborately enveloped in white satin, with, Campaspe thought, a good deal of the air of a superdreadnought in attendance on a masquerade garden-party. Across the floor, in the grateful vicinity of a lady with pale golden-green hair, almost the shade of sea-foam, Paul hovered. She caught a glimpse of Hubert Miles and his wife, and of the Duquesa de Azul, who was said to be déclassée, but who went everywhere in spite of her noisome reputation. The Duquesa, Campaspe reflected, had chien. Nearer at hand were the towering blond, Frederic Richards, who was holding an exhibition at Knoedler's, and Florizel Hammond, whose chief claim to attention was the fact that he had constituted himself a species of walking gazette. Watching him stroke his feeble moustache, Campaspe noted that it was characteristic of him that he should wear an evening suit of dark blue, the trousers of which were copiously pleated near the waist-line.

The song was over, and after the applause subsided, the buzz of conversation began again.

Mystical, drawled Lalla, damned mystical, what?

Where's the old girl stow her whisky? Jack demanded.

Campaspe wondered if they both meant the same thing. She also marvelled that she had come at all. In this languid, disinterested mood, she listened to Florizel Hammond relating to a friend the extraordinary details of a new and celebrated divorce case.

She caught him very neatly, the youth was remarking. Gene came home one night, after an absence that needed explaining, and told her that he had dined with Bud Wetmore. Gertie called Bud up immediately and asked if he had served asparagus for dinner. Armed with Bud's negative response, she forced a confession from Gene.

At the end of the tale the spinner caught Campaspe's eye.

Hello, 'paspe, he said. How did you like the singing?

It made me a little nervous, she replied.

What I say is why sing that tripe at all? Girls are going abroad now to learn to sing Wagner and Debussy and Verdi, while the rest of the world has stopped listening to these birds. Why don't they stay at home and learn to sing George Gershwin—if they can? There's a career in that.

Bravo, Florio! Lalla applauded him, striking him on the back with her fan of rude hawk feathers.

Mrs. Pollanger was bearing down on the group.

Campaspe, she wheezed, like an asthmatic walrus, I am delighted! I was afraid you wouldn't come. And Lalla, too!

We dined together tonight, Campaspe explained, and Jack didn't get enough whisky.

There are *barrels* in the library.

Catching the last word, Jack disappeared. Campaspe permitted her mind to wander while Isabel chattered. From the ball-room the strains of the Limehouse Blues drifted down. Campaspe recognized the band as Paul Whiteman's. Florizel bubbled on—how did he find out so much?

It's her first novel. Have you read it? Well, it's as rotten as you'd expect. Agarista sent it to a publisher who owned a dog and the dog chewed up the manuscript before anybody had a chance to look it over. The publisher was forced to write her, of course, that he would accept her beautiful prose. Naturally, the story was too good to keep, and later it leaked out. Now she says that when she has written another masterpiece, she will urge her publisher to please refer it to his mastiff again.

Campaspe was aware of Laura, making her delicate way across the room in her direction. In W. H. Mallock's The New Republic, it will be recalled, Mr. Rose carried a scrap of artistic cretonne in his pocket when he visited an ugly house, as a kind of æsthetic smelling-salts. To serve a similar requirement of her own nature, Laura, when she permitted herself to attend a function that she considered in any sense vulgar, always wore an unbecoming dress. It gave her, no doubt, a feeling of security even in the midst of a presumably smirched, social atmosphere.

O, Campaspe, I'm so glad you're here, Laura cried. George *would* come—he says it's as good as a trip to Montmartre—and so I came too, but I'm. . .

Again Campaspe was finding it impossible to listen. It was a comparatively simple matter to talk to Laura by interjecting a monosyllable now and then, and at the same time overhear what her neighbours were saying.

Arabella Munson is coming back to America, Florizel announced to Lalla. If she dances here with as few clothes as formerly I propose for the motto across the façade of the theatre where she appears, The old lady shows her medals.

A few feet in front of her, his back towards her, stood a tall, distinguished man, held in the merciless grip of Isabel Pollanger's concentrated attention.

How do you go about constructing your plots, situations, and characters, Mr. Johns?

So it was the guest of honour. Campaspe heard his response, suave enough in tone: I don't know that I go about it at all.

I mean, his hostess persevered, do you develop the atmosphere of your books consciously or unconsciously?

If you want to know whether I work when I am awake, the answer is that I do.

Isabel persisted: O, now do tell me, do you believe in working regularly so many hours each day or do you wait until the spirit moves you?

If I waited for anything, I'd still be waiting.

Do you work fast or slowly?

Fast *and* slowly.

Is it hard or easy?

Hard *and* easy.

Does it help you to talk over your ideas before you write them?

I have never tried it.

Do you like to meet other noted authors or do you prefer not to?

There are so few of us that it's not much use protesting.

What kind of writing do you think is the most fun?

Writing cheques.

What has proved the most popular with your public?

At this point an overwhelming sense of pity surged into the breast of Campaspe Lorillard. She turned away from Laura.

Isabel, she broke in, will you introduce me to Mr. Johns?

His eyes thanked her and then travelled caressingly down her rose and grey splendour until they met her satined feet. At the same time she took him in: thick, white hair, an interesting and sympathetic expression, behind which lurked a suggestion of bitterness and even cruelty.

My wife, Mrs. Lorillard, he explained, rather than introduced, a little woman in blue beside him whom Campaspe noticed for the first time. She had the air of a person eager to run errands, desirous only of serving as a buffer between her handsome and talented husband and the aggressive world.

I think you need a drink. Campaspe smiled at him.

Do you know where there is one?

In the lib—Mrs. Pollanger began to recite.

Excuse us, then, for a moment. They spoke in unison.

Mrs. Pollanger waved her fan. Come back, you clever man and tell me *all* about your new book!

What a woman! Gareth exclaimed. She looks like a footbath on wheels. Did you see all those diamonds on her. . . ? As though Queen Mary had belted the gas-works with her royal stomacher!

In the corridor stood the singer of La Chevelure, the nervous prey of Augusta Illinois, the celebrated soprano.

You're too fat, Claire, the Illinois proclaimed, to sing in public.

Claire Madrilena met her tormentor's eye. I've needed my body so little in my career, she retorted.

Pretty good. The ubiquitous Florizel Hammond was nudging Campaspe. Pretty fair. The Illinois has ostermoored her way into four opera houses, but no one has ever before expressed the fact so neatly.

Hello, 'paspe, Jack Draycott hailed them as they entered the library. *Hello!* You've trapped the lion!

He was thirsty, too.

I've got a bottle of fine old brandy, 1804, somewhere, Mr. Humphry Pollanger was explaining. Would you care to sample it?

Would we care to? Jack echoed mockingly. Bring it forth, old chap.

As his host departed on his mission of cheer, Jack demanded, Who was that fellow, 'paspe?

Mrs. Lorillard did not reply. Fascinated, she was listening again to the indefatigable Florizel Hammond.

Speaking of brandy, that one was saying, Eddie Blue has got it cached all over his place down at Montauk Point, brandy and Burgundy and everything you can think of, all the best years, too. He was the only man in America to take prohibition seriously. Two months before the amendment went into effect he put a fortune into booze. Immediately thereafter he was confronted with the difficulty of discovering a place where he might store it safely. He solved the problem by hiring workmen to dig twelve hours into the earth on selected and charted spots on his estate. He figured, if it took a man twelve hours to dig a hole, that, after it was filled up, it would take a thief just as long and, as there are not twelve hours of darkness in any day, it was not likely that he could dig without being observed. He instituted further schemes for protection. He caused some of the caves to be filled with poison-gas and he stationed two men in the tower which caps his house to cover the prospect with machine-guns. Of course, any one can buy all the stuff he wants now, but if you want vintages and assured purity you have to drink at Eddie's. He won't even sell a bottle, although he possesses enough to keep three generations of his family stewed the year round.

I witnessed a most curious form of drinking the other night, Gareth Johns remarked. A mother nursed her child during Aguglia's performance of The Daughter of Jorio at the Thalia. I watched the baby, sucking, prattling, cooing, patting her mother's cheek during the tragic scenes. The mother's eyes dilated with horror. Would the child, I wondered, drink in some of her mother's emotion with the milk?

Florizel added a variation to the theme. D'Annunzio, he announced, advises his disciples to drink gallons of black coffee to keep them awake. He tells them that if they go to sleep they may miss something.

Campaspe asked herself again why she had come to this house. She dispatched Florizel on an errand. Invite Madame Madrilena to join us.

Will you wait for the 1804 brandy? she demanded of the author by her side, or. . . ? She waved her arm in the direction of the table, covered with an embroidered Italian linen cloth, on which liqueur bottles were ranged in the form of a rainbow, while champagne, whisky, a bowl of military punch, bottles of soda, and glasses and goblets of every description kept them company. Two men in uniform were constantly employed behind this improvised bar.

Gareth smiled. I'll wait for the brandy, he replied.

Florizel reappeared with the contralto in tow.

Do secure for me, she urged her escort after the presentations, one of those evil buns. You have such expressive feet, Mrs. Lorillard, she went on.

I'm admiring your sables, Campaspe countered.

This cloak was of a splendour before it wore out in the direction of the sit-upon. Now, it resembles a rabbit who has had an extensive career. Ah! thank you! She nibbled the bun. After singing I am pantophagous.

Do you think it's a moral act to take off so many vocal clothes?

Madame Madrilena rolled her eyes. It's good for these people, she explained. They're so middle-class. Look at those flowers—she pointed to the epergne on the table—even the flowers are middle-class. Utterly lacking in passion. I think I'd like to sing for them, too. They need a dash of sex!

I should think you are the one to give it to them, Gareth suggested.

I wish I might. I have only men to experiment on. Why were men made for women? They understand them so little.

I have heard of substitutes, Florizel muttered.

Mr. Humphry Pollanger had returned, carefully bearing a carafe half-full of an amber fluid. Here it is! he cried.

Don't crow too loud, old rooster, Jack counselled. There won't be enough for the crowd, you know.

He's pouring it out in the largest goblets, thank God! Florizel noted. That's the way to serve good brandy, just a little in the bottom so that the fumes fill the glass with an exquisite bouquet, but no one in this country seems to know it.

There isn't any good brandy in this country, unless this is it, declared Paul, who had joined them.

Silent now, each with glass to his nose, they savoured the rich aroma.

Great stuff, old fellow! Jack's was the first appreciation. Napoleonic, you said?

Yes, I think so. Mr. Humphry Pollanger's face was the façade of his delight. No one had ever before paid him so much attention.

They all took a sip.

Um.

Um.

Um.

Um.

George, come here.

Laura's husband attached himself to the group.

Marvellous.

Delicious.

Exquise.

An expression of doubt shadowed the face of Mr. Humphry Pollanger. He held the carafe at arm's length between his eyes and a lamp. Then he sniffed at the unstopped neck. I'm not so sure. . . he explained hesitantly. There were two carafes on the shelf. One of them certainly contains 1804 brandy. The other holds some whisky left over from our bootlegger's latest call.

Don't worry, old chap. Jack gave his unrecognized host a slap on the shoulder. Can't you tell brandy when you drink it? Cognac, fine champagne, that's what it is!

I'm not so sure. . . I think this is the whisky!

Of *course,* this is brandy, George asserted.

Paul executed a few steps of the Charleston while Mr. Pollanger made another hurried journey to his store of supplies. Presently he returned with a second carafe. He held the two to the light together, comparing them one with the other. Precisely the same colour, he muttered in despair.

Well, just to convince you, I'll try a little of the other, was Jack's handsome offer. He extended his empty goblet. This time he did not wait to enjoy the bouquet. He swallowed the contents in one gulp. Whisky! he sputtered. The first was brandy.

I think, Mr. Pollanger put forward timidly, after sampling a drink from the new bottle, that *this* is the brandy.

Whisky!

Brandy!

Let me try the first carafe again, Jack urged.

Madame Madrilena was working on the second. I think this *is* the brandy, she averred.

Let *me* try the new kind, George suggested. Who is that man? he whispered interrogatively to Campaspe.

Campaspe was experimenting with the second bottle. Why, they're both the same! she announced.

I think I can tell cognac when I drink it, Jack insisted hotly. The first was cognac, the second Scotch.

What's the row? Lalla, arriving, demanded.

Don't tell her, Paul urged, before we get her unbiased opinion. He offered her a drink from the first carafe.

What is it? Florizel inquired eagerly.

What's what?

What you're drinking.

Scotch, of course, Lalla replied.

Why, Lalla, can't you tell brandy when you drink it?

Brandy! Nonsense, Jack! You're so squiffy you'd call absinthe brandy.

Give her a taste of the other stuff.

Scotch, Lalla announced, even more firmly than before.

Madame Madrilena was occupied. I think they're both cognac, was her new decision.

Campaspe smiled. Whatever they are, she repeated, they're both the same.

The second carafe contains the cognac, Mr. Pollanger persisted, almost as if some one had hurt him.

Who *is* that man? Lalla demanded of George in a whisper.

The *first* is cognac. I ought to be able to know cognac, Jack cried. Napoleonic cognac, at that.

Don't be an ass, Jack. They're both Scotch.

I think they're both fine champagne, Madame Madrilena insisted.

I've an idea, Campaspe suggested. Let Jack select them blindfold.

Splendid!

Great!

Just the thing!

Jack, bursting with pride over his capacity for distinguishing tastes, assented to this test willingly enough. Lalla bound the scarf around his eyes, and saw to it that it was efficacious in limiting his vision.

Brandy! Jack cried, after his first sip.

But, Paul expostulated, that's from the *second* carafe.

Jack tore off the bandage. You've mixed them up, he swore. That's from the first.

Don't be an ass, Jack, Lalla implored him. They're both Scotch.

One of 'em is brandy. . . Poor Mr. Pollanger was ready to weep. . . I'm certain one of 'em is brandy.

I've got it! cried George. We'll ask the barkeeps. They're sure to know.

Great! Paul encouraged the idea.

Though it won't make the least difference what they say, because both carafes contain Scotch, Lalla inserted.

One of 'em is brandy. I think it's the second, Mr. Pollanger politely demurred. Even in the throes of anguish over being contradicted, he recalled with some pleasure that never before had he carried on so extended a conversation with any of his wife's guests.

Who is that man? Madame Madrilena demanded feverishly, and then muttered sullenly, Cognac!

The servants readily agreed to decide the matter, but when George handed them the carafes it was discovered that both were empty.

A quarter of an hour later, Gareth and Campaspe were sitting in a small reception-room, which they occupied alone, on a curly maple settle, more picturesque than comfortable. In the distance, Paul Whiteman's band was playing Mama Loves Papa. The castenets snarled, the saxophone scolded, the banjos barked. Campaspe had thrown off her cloak of flamingo feathers, and was fingering the choker of moonstones that encircled her throat.

We haven't discussed your books yet, she remarked, not without malice.

Don't! he groaned. Everybody upstairs talked about them. If only they'd say something. He brightened. Maybe you would!

Campaspe's smile was sardonic. I haven't read them, she began, but I can ask you questions. Do you believe in working regularly so many hours each day or do you wait until the spirit moves you?

Devil! Madrilena was right. You *have* expressive feet. I'd like to write a book about your feet. He was examining the objects of his interest.

Smooth-shod.

What a title! May I borrow it?

Campaspe yawned. At this juncture Frederic Richards, accompanied by the girl with sea-foam hair, passed through the room.

Have you seen his drawings?

Whose drawings?

That was Frederic Richards.

You don't say. And the girl with the green hair?

I don't know her.

And where do you buy your gowns?

I have a little woman who comes in.

Chéruit or Jenny's her name, I suppose.

How do you go about constructing your plots, situations, and characters?

By spending as much of this evening as possible with you!

I was convinced you drew from the life. Do you work fast or slow?

Fast. I hope some day you will give me the opportunity to be unfaithful to you.

Laura, an anxious expression distorting her features, now hovered in the doorway. She brightened when she observed Campaspe.

O, Campaspe, have you seen George? I want to go home.

Saw him half-an-hour ago in the library. Have you met Mr. Johns?

O, Mr. Johns, I'm so glad! There is a question I want to ask you. I hope you will *understand*. I read Two on the Seine and I appreciate the *style* and the way you have drawn the characters and the *art* of it all, but why do you devote your genius to such sordid subjects?

My subjects choose me, Gareth replied. I have nothing to do with the selection.

Laura evidently regarded this as an attempt at cocoonery. But I don't see. . . she went on. If you would seek out subjects that would please people. . .

Probably then, Campaspe finished the sentence for her, his books would stop selling.

I think, Laura announced with dignity, that I shall look up George in the library.

Have you been to supper yet?

I don't want any supper. I want to go home.

Bestowing a frigid bow on the novelist, she wandered off.

Well, I do, Campaspe, rising, averred.

Do what?

Want supper. Come along and feed me.

Like the lady, Gareth protested, I'm in no mood for supper.

I suppose, Campaspe suggested gravely, the question Laura asked you is the one you hear most frequently.

She was amazed by the suddenness with which he threw off his mask of irony. Pricked in his vanity, he became as garrulous as a schoolgirl.

Every day! Every hour! Letters! Letters! All inquiring why I don't write about something else. I write about what I know, in the way I feel about it. It doesn't seem to occur to the crowd that it is possible for an author to believe that life is largely without excuse, that if there is a God he conducts the show aimlessly, if not, indeed, maliciously, that men and women run around automatically seeking escapes from their troubles and outlets for their lusts. The crowd is still more incensed when an author who believes these things refuses to write about them seriously.

Recently, in a London music hall, I saw an act which enthralled me. The curtain rose to disclose a house in process of construction. Three workmen were on the job. They did not speak a word. They indicated the symbols by pantomime. Their every action was ridiculously futile, ending in disaster. If a carpenter ascended a scaffold, the scaffold broke, giving him a hard fall of ten feet and undoing all the labour accomplished by his comrades; when one of the fellows began to plaster, he presently dropped into the mixing vat. So it went on, and whenever a man met with an accident his predicament was ignored by his companions. He was forced to extricate himself. As the curtain descended, the house, far from being in a further state of construction, was nearly demolished. The audience characteristically shrieked with laughter at this act, but I, for the same reason that they laughed, was on the verge of tears. This performance seemed to me exactly like life as we live it.

Don't you find it rather absurd to write books about the futility of life? Campaspe demanded.

Gareth grinned. Not at all, he replied. I write my books to prove how futile life is in a vain effort to forget how futile it is!

Campaspe studied the novelist's face with more interest. You do not appear to have many illusions, she volunteered.

Illusions! It would be pleasant if nobody had any. Only the thoroughly disillusioned expect nothing from others. They make life slightly more human. But all of us have illusions, or sentimental moods, which amount to the same thing. . . My God! he went on, tossing his thick hair back with one hand, have you ever observed that after a few cocktails you can listen to a banal waltz played in a dimly lighted theatre and feel as sweet or good or true or noble as the most fatuous moron ever felt? I always become sentimental after I drink cocktails and music aggravates the sensation.

Have you written a book about that? If you have I'll read it.

It's damned difficult to get any intangible thought into a book. Anything subtle is almost impossible to get into a book. Yet that is the only thing I want to do. My reward is that after I get it in—or at least think I get it in—nobody knows it's there, unless I tell them. An old English actor, one George Bartley, said of the British theatre-going public: You must first tell them that you are going to do so and so; you must then tell them that you are doing it, and then that you have done it; and then, by God, *perhaps* they will understand you! Well, the same thing is true of the novel-reading public, but I don't tell them, and they don't understand, but they read me anyway. Perhaps I should be satisfied.

Campaspe was silent, but it was obvious that she was listening, and after a moment he went on: The incoherence of life has always interested me, the appalling disconnection. We wander around alone, each with his own thoughts, his own ideas. We connect only in flashes.

Only in flashes?

Yes. It usually happens in this way: abruptly, quite unreasonably, one individual unconsciously—it's always unconsciously—produces an effect, a chemical change, let us call it, in another person with whom he comes in contact. This phenomenon in itself creates enough energy so that presently still others are affected. Wider and wider sweep the circles, like the circles created by the tossing of a pebble into a lake, until at last they dissipate, and the lake becomes placid again.

Campaspe regarded him with an interrogative eye.

Or, to put it figuratively in another fashion, he continued, you must think of a group of people in terms of a packet of firecrackers. You ignite the first cracker and the flash fires the fuse of the second, and so on, until, after a series of crackling detonations, the whole bunch has exploded, and nothing survives but a few torn and scattered bits of paper, blackened with powder. On the other hand, if you fail to apply the match, the bunch remains a collection of separate entities, having no connection one with any other. Explosions which create relationships are sporadic and terminating, but if you avoid the explosions you perdurably avoid intercourse. And now, he said, I think I'm hungry.

At this moment, Mrs. Johns appeared in the doorway. Gareth glared at her.

Gareth dear, she urged, you know that you have so much to do tomorrow.

Can't you see that I'm taking Mrs. Lorillard to supper? was the great author's impatient rejoinder.

That man from the Saturday Evening Post is coming at nine o'clock, she reminded him.

To hell with him!

Why don't you come to supper with us, Campaspe suggested, and then take your husband home?

Before this invitation, Gareth immediately became more reasonable. There, Bella, he cajoled her, I'll be with you shortly. I've something more to say to Mrs. Lorillard.

You won't be too long, dear, the little woman pleaded before she awkwardly retired.

Always trying to make me go home, Gareth grumbled.

She probably knows what's good for you.

Good Lord, yes, but I don't want to do what's good for me.

In the supper-room upstairs, they were joined by Florizel Hammond who, at evening entertainments, invariably divided his time between the rooms where food and drink were served.

You author chaps must get the low-down on all of us at these bull-fights, he opened up on Gareth.

We'd like to, Gareth replied.

Well, God knows, there's enough. Take a few notes. What do you want, 'paspe, a lobster sandwich or some Smithfield ham?

Both, Campaspe replied.

I thought *I* was taking you to supper, Gareth grumbled, as Florizel wandered away to execute his commission.

I asked you to, Campaspe smiled at him, but you were so long in accepting my invitation that I thought I might starve if I waited for you to fill my plate. Why don't you share supper with Florizel and me?

The large room was pleasantly full. Some, holding their plates, ate standing. Others sat, while they rested their plates on the arms of their chairs. In the centre of the room, on a great round table, heaped with dishes, food steamed in casseroles. A number of waiters in uniform, bearing trays laden with glasses of champagne, solemnly passed from guest to guest. The odour of Vague Souvenir soared above the confusion of other aromas.

Have you heard about Dennis Cahill? Florizel, returning with heaped plates, demanded, and without waiting for a reply went on, Well, you know, before he was married he was all mixed up in his subconscious—and every other way, too, but he wasn't aware of that *yet,* although his friends had their suspicions. So he went to Dr. Leonard and was psyched and all his suppressed desires were pulled out into the open, but when he married he discovered that these released desires weren't strong enough to see him through, and so he resorted to goat glands.

And lived happily ever after? Gareth queried.

My dear, you're wrong. They won't last six months. He'll be taking the Steinach treatment before the year's out. There's a tragic anecdote for you, Johns.

Too tragic, I fear. The public demands pleasant stories, I'm learning.

The group was interrupted by a dark beauty in flaming velvet who verbally assaulted the author without the formality of an introduction.

I just loved Two on the Seine, she avowed. I love all your books. What was that other one? O, yes, Black Oxen.

That is my own favourite, Gareth remarked.

Florizel, who is the girl? Campaspe inquired, as soon as the novelist's admirer was out of ear-shot.

That's Mahalah Wiggins, the actress.

Where does she act?

In an old-fashioned piece of furniture with four posts. Have you heard. . . Florizel continued without pause. . . about Isabel in Venice, the city where men fiddle while women burn? She embarked in a gondola, tossed a ring into the Grand Canal, and announced, Now, I am a dogaressa!

Campaspe again was not listening. Her nerves were playing her odd tricks. She had the impression of a presence in the room, a presence that was affecting her emotions in some disturbing way. Like a lone hunter, in the depths of the jungle, suddenly instinctively conscious that somewhere nearby, behind the screen of green that obstructs his vision, a man-eating tiger lies crouched for a spring, she awaited, not without trepidation, the moment when the unknown force should choose to become visible. Waited, icy cold, and *alone*. . . Presently, she saw the *other*. Straight across the room, in uniform, like the rest of the servants, bearing a tray, he was moving, as yet unaware, directly towards her. Unaware, and yet uneasy. Silver, silver, the faint tinkling of bells, and a sickening, unfamiliar odour, an overpowering scent. Dizzy, she closed her eyes, and took two uncertain steps. Forcing herself, with every particle of will at her command to open them again, she stared ahead of her. And now, at last, he too saw her, and the secret she read in his eyes provided her with a new torment. Before, however, she was able to move forward or to speak, Gunnar averted his gaze, pivoted on his heel, and hurled the laden platter through a window, shattering the pane from sash to sill. Without hesitating a second, in one prodigiously agile leap, he followed the missile into the outside blackness.

Instantly, she regained her poise, resaw her companions, but now the appearance of the crowd was altered almost beyond recognition. The ladies screamed. Two men rushed to the aperture. Good God! Thirty feet! There's a perfectly good window gone! Mrs. Pollanger, a tragic barrel, held the centre of the floor and raised her hand. Tell them to stop the music! she cried hoarsely. Tell them to stop the music!

Twelve

Miss Pinchon was a woman with a practical turn of mind. During the limited period in which she had been going out as governess she had put aside major sums from her modest wages, certainly with no definite plan in view, but just as certainly with an ideal, however abstract. Still comparatively young, she cherished the steadfast intention of maintaining herself, in the near future, on a more independent level. The exact date of departure, until recently, had remained hazy and unfixed. Only the week before, indeed, she had not yet determined upon the precise hour she should choose to embark on a more personal enterprise, nor had she selected the enterprise, but the crossing of her trail by the Brothers Steel and a casual remark dropped by Campaspe Lorillard had sown the seed of reflection in her mind, seed that found fertilization in the basic desire that already impregnated her brain. One night the little governess lay awake for hours, at intervals repeating aloud to herself, Why not? Why not? and figuratively snapping her fingers.

The following afternoon, as soon as she was free from the lessons she was engaged to impart to Consuelo, Miss Pinchon paid a visit to the Public Library where she devoted herself to a more or less extensive examination of curious works by Ouspensky and Arthur E. Waite. Further, she drew up a list from the catalogue of volumes on Hindu philosophy and noted down the titles of pamphlets dealing with Gurdjieff, Jaques-Dalcroze, and Einstein. A few of these she later purchased for home study. Within a week, a week of intensive research, she had evolved, with plagiarism here and there, and a limited use of the imagination, a philosophy of acrobatics which would suit her purpose and which, she was convinced, not unjustifiably, would make her fortune. Deep breathing while standing on the head during the simultaneous consideration of the ultimate oneness of God with humankind, the essential co-ordination of the waving left arm with the soul, and the identity of the somersault with the freedom of the will were a few of the attractive determining principles in this new mental-physical science which she dubbed, following the fashion of previous innovators along these lines, Pinchon's Prophylactic Plan. Having established thoroughly in her own mind the essential tenets of this novel cult, having, indeed, entrusted them to the pages of a large note-book, the contents of which at some day in the future she intended to commit to print, Miss Pinchon took a second step. At the close of one of Consuelo's lessons with the Brothers Steel, she astonished the mountebanks with a request for an interview. This, naturally, was granted, however radical they may have regarded such conduct on the part of a lady whose manner hitherto had been completely self-effacing.

Miss Pinchon, confronted with the task of converting pagans, made no futile attempt during this interview to explain the lights and shades of her system. She did not read aloud the statement of her principles. She did not, indeed, avow openly that she had a system. She began by mentioning a salary which, as the number of pupils enrolled increased, might be advanced accordingly. Then she sketched lightly the advantages of muscular training for the young, combined with—and here she drew her descriptive picture with the faintest line—certain mental and spiritual exercises. Lastly, she suggested that her position and its corresponding influence—as she felt this section of her discourse to be the most telling, she exaggerated its effect, drawing upon her imagination for salient details—would be the magnet which would attract the pupils.

While Miss Pinchon explained her plan, the twins, in identical postures, left hand on hip, right hand stroking moustache, sat quietly agape on their bench, their eyes popping from the sockets. It remained for Mrs. Hugo, who had listened with a more sympathetic absorption, to welcome the idea with enthusiasm, and to speak the first word after Miss Pinchon had spoken her last.

I say, do it, she urged flatly.

I dunno. Could we? queried Robin.

That's it, was Hugo's dubious contribution.

It beats vaudeville. . . Mrs. Hugo's excitement was contagious. . . You're always fussin' about bookin', always wonderin' who's goin' to crib your act, and you're always out of town eatin' punk food in rotten boardin'-houses. When Miss Consuelo first come here I said it was a chance. Here's your chance, boys, was my words. Well, here it is. Take it.

It looks like it, mother, Robin put forward feebly.

It looks all right, Hugo remarked doubtfully.

It *is* all right, Miss Pinchon asseverated warmly. You leave it to me and you'll see.

Having secured the consent of the brothers, none the less binding because it was somewhat unhearty—the governess belonged to that group of persons who believe that one should take immediate advantage of a permission, even when it is given with bad grace, lest it may be withdrawn—Miss Pinchon secured the lease of a hall on East Fiftieth Street, and left an order with a painter on First Avenue, whose ordinary occupation was the decoration of Jacobean chests and Queen Anne tables in the Chinese style, for certain charts on which figures were to be drawn, the arms and legs in certain attitudes she had observed the brothers assume during the course of their evolutions, accompanied by quotations from the Cabala and the Upanishads. Next, she called on George Everest at his office.

George felt regret at losing Miss Pinchon's services as governess for Consuelo and Eugenia, but he reflected that the unpleasant duty of discovering a substitute would devolve upon Laura, and he was so amused by the initiative displayed by the little woman in front of him and by the nature of her plan that he not only gave her permission to use his name in her circulars—had not, indeed, the course of instruction, even shorn of the further mental and spiritual attachments, proved of immense benefit to his daughter?—but also presented her with a cheque for one thousand dollars, averring that he desired to invest in the scheme himself, at least to the degree to which this small amount would entitle him.

Miss Pinchon was now fully fortified to experiment with her plan in a practical manner. She resigned from her position, after a most disagreeable scene with Mrs. Everest, during which Laura had implied—she had not exactly said—that the governess must be mad, established herself in her new quarters, and issued cards which read as follows:

Miss Emmeline Pinchon
announces the opening of her school
for the propagation of
her own mental-physical method

PINCHON'S PROPHYLACTIC PLAN
at 107 East Fiftieth Street

Lessons in class: Two lessons a week for ten weeks: $200
Private lessons: Two lessons a week for ten weeks: $400
Reference: Mr. George Everest Telephone: Sahara 6897

Two days after the cards had been sent out she received three replies. Interviews followed. When the school opened she found herself with nine class and three private pupils. Hiram Mason's son, Ira Barber's little girl, and Maida Sonsconsett were all included in the list of registrants. It was not long before Lalla Draycott sent her eight-year old son. It began to appear fairly certain that the next generation of New York society would be able to form pyramids to equal the best that could be created by travelling troupes of wild Arabs. Mrs. Pollanger talked of giving a Pinchon evening for the demonstration of the new method, and the New York Times devoted a full page in its Sunday Magazine to an analysis of it.

Meanwhile Consuelo continued her private education with the Brothers Steel at their own gymnasium, accompanied now by Miss Elizabeth Graves, the new governess, an Englishwoman whom Laura had selected primarily because she did not appear to be the possessor of an inventive mind. Laura thought she might be able to keep her at least until she found time to discover a house on the far-east side, a project suggested to her by a casual remark of Campaspe.

Consuelo nourished reasons of her own for not desiring to join the new school, although, in an impersonal way, she admired Miss Pinchon and was sufficiently appreciative of her spirit of aggressive determination. It was not difficult for her to persuade her father to permit her to please herself in this respect, as George had long ago decided to allow Consuelo to do anything she wanted to do within reason. She seems, he explained to Laura, not entirely to his wife's satisfaction, to know so much better what to do and how to do it than the rest of us.

To Consuelo, however, the lesson-hours brought no pleasure. They constituted, rather, a severe penance, a means to an end which was not too apparent either to her parents or to her professors. Occasionally, a certain laxity and lassitude betrayed itself in her actions, even while she was in the gymnasium. Ordinarily, on the contrary, she displayed an energy, a grim intensity, which soon carried her beyond the elements of the art, to gain the technique of which she was unswerving in her desire. Two considerations accounted for her relentless perseverance, her consistent attention to her masters' schooling: one, her long-since, self-confessed adoration for Gunnar, to whom, in imagination, at any rate, she always felt near when she stood in the room where he had lived and worked, and whom, if she did not expect, she certainly hoped to see return one day, to reappear in this spot which in a sense was sacred to his memory; the other, her ambition to do what he did as well as he did it.

One day her audible sighs caught and held the attention of the sympathetic and motherly Mrs. Hugo, who was beginning to feel for this child more than an ordinary amount of affection, now that she had been the means of introducing the brothers to an occupation which apparently would feed and clothe and house them indefinitely, for while the vaudeville world demanded fresh talent, young and agile limbs, every new decade, the academic world, the philosophical and scientific world, appeared to be open to them so long as they were able to indicate, however feebly, the proper gestures leading to the acquirement of this long and difficult art.

What is it, dearie? the good woman inquired.

Nothing, Consuelo replied, but she sighed again. She was sitting, half-reclining, on the bench so often occupied by the brothers. She still retained the costume of her practice-hour and her usually pale face was flushed from exertion on the parallel bars. Outside, the day was bright and cold, and the sunlight invaded the great chamber, together with the chill, but Consuelo was oblivious to the sensations created by either.

When, she demanded plaintively, after a pause, will he come back?

Who, dearie?

Why, Gunnar, of course?

Hush, dear. We don't know where he is no more'n you do. He's gone away. He may never come back.

This adjuration reminded Consuelo unpleasantly of a similar remark that her mother had made, perhaps more naïvely, when she had asked news of a favourite uncle. Later, she had learned that the uncle was dead. Somehow, she did not feel at all convinced that Gunnar was dead, although certainly, this was the impression that Mrs. Hugo, however involuntarily, had conveyed. If Gunnar were dead, she assured herself on the testimony of her day-dreams, he would return to her in a vision, as a knight in silver armour, a spirit in mother-of-pearl mail, driving a chariot of fire. No, she could not but hold the unshakable belief that Gunnar would come back alive, come back, moreover, to this spot.

Nevertheless, she sighed again, remarking only, He will return.

At home, too, her melancholy was the occasion for comment. Laura was really more than usually anxious about the child, ascribing this new condition to the influence of those terrible acrobats.

Nonsense, George disagreed. They are doing her good. Consuelo never had colour before. She hasn't been seen reading a book for weeks. Something else must be the trouble. Perhaps she misses Emmeline

Pinchon, or perhaps you are not feeding her properly, or perhaps it's the growing pains of adolescence.

Laura metaphorically threw up her hands and began to talk about a new house she had discovered in the proper district.

Never in the habit of confiding in her parents, Consuelo made no exception in this instance. They, on their part, refrained from asking her direct questions. They were, even George was, a little afraid of this prodigy that they called their daughter, a little alarmed by the burning mentality which seemed to consume her and keep her alive at the same time. Consuelo loved Eugenia after her fashion, but with her, too, she preserved a dignified silence. To her sister, indeed, Eugenia was only a child whose sympathy would be of small avail.

Once or twice she considered the advisability of a visit to Campaspe, but for some reason which she could not make clear even to herself she distrusted Campaspe in this matter. Her instinct even told her that Campaspe had in some way been responsible for Gunnar's disappearance. She had heard, not without bitter astonishment and a deep feeling of resentment that she had not been present to beg him to stay, of Gunnar's sudden leap from the window of the supper-room at Mrs. Pollanger's, and it had not escaped her attention that some one had mentioned Campaspe's presence in the room at the time the evacuation occurred. No, she decided, it was better to struggle alone than to confide in Campaspe at this difficult juncture.

The child then was leading two lives, one in which she strengthened her muscles and acquired agility at the gymnasium of the Brothers Steel, another, in which she dreamed, fully awake, of her effulgent hero. She often fancied him coming for her, lifting her tenderly from her seat in the window and bearing her down a ladder of silken ropes to his waiting car, in which he whirled her swiftly away to an eternity of happiness. A second vision pictured his approach in an aeroplane, which skimmed near enough the earth to enable him to snatch her up to him for a journey of fierce joy through the skies.

And always these fantasies ended with the same self-assuring hope, He will return, and she would spread her arms wide, and whisper to the clouds that passed her window, Come back, Gunnar. I am waiting for you.

Thirteen

As time passed, Paul fell so completely under the spell of the charm of the world of affairs that he seriously began to consider the advisability of following the general custom of taking on a mistress.

I mustn't be too marked, he averred to George Everest from the rich brown leather of a couch at the Moloch Club. Everybody else down here is keeping somebody and I seem to be out of it. John Armstrong warns me against stenographers. What do you say?

Well, old man, George roared back at him, what do *you* say?

Paul grinned. For the moment he was not prepared to say anything more. The idea, although it had been revolving vaguely in his head, had just assumed formal expression. The next day, however, he did not lunch at the club as usual, and a little later in the afternoon, Florizel Hammond reported that he had squinted at Paul in the company of a cutie at Fraunces' Tavern. Thereafter, Paul and his cutie became the subjects for a good deal of ribald gibing around Wall Street. They had been observed dining at Voisin's and the Crillon; they had been seen motoring on the Boston Post Road at a late hour. Paul, indeed, it was beginning to be recognized, had at last become a regular business man.

Entering the Moloch Club one day, alone, he was greeted with applause.

Aren't you going to introduce us?

How's Delilah?

Growing up, eh? was Jack Draycott's interrogative comment, while Florizel Hammond burst into song:

She had a dark and roving eye,
And her hair hung down in ring-a-lets,
A nice girl,
A decent girl,
But one of the rakish kind!

The crowd took up the refrain. Even George Everest, busy at the ticker, managed to get in with

A nice girl,
A decent girl,

while one white-bearded old fellow whose paunch and buttocks occupied fully two-thirds of a broad couch, giving him the appearance of a prosperous Easter egg, bawled out in a deep bass that drowned all the others:

But one of the rakish kind!

Paul received this bantering with disarming good-nature. It added, indeed, to his happiness, causing him to wonder whether it was business or his brunette which he preferred. One, assuredly, gave edge to the other; even his relations with Vera were now sufficiently oblique to interest him.

I hope it isn't a stenographer, Paul, John Armstrong hinted darkly. You know what I told you.

What *does* she do, anyway, Paul? Jack Draycott demanded.

Yes, what *does* she do? the crowd inquired in chorus.

Paul grinned. She paints, he replied.

Paints! Good God, they all do! Florizel howled. Paints! That's a good one! Another song had occurred to him:

Her lips are two bumpers of clary,
Who drinks of them sure he'll miscarry—
Her breasts of delight
Are two bumpers of white,
And her eyes are two cups of canary!

Wintergreen Waterbury was not actually a painter. To be sure, she cherished ambitions, based on no known talents, to wield the brush, but her career, up to date, had been that of artists' model. She had frequently been heard to remark, however, while Harrison Fisher or Rolf Armstrong was engaged in making a replica of her pretty face, I could do that if I wanted to, or You'll have to get a new model soon, I'm going to open a studio of my own. A curious fact was that, although her fresh, innocuous face, her even, white teeth, her saccharine smile, and her dark hair had graced the covers of half the popular magazines half-a-dozen times each, a state of affairs which convinced her that she was as celebrated in her own sphere as Gloria Swanson in hers, not one of the men in the Moloch Club had recognized her, notwithstanding the fact that her portrait had appeared on the very periodicals they were most in the habit of reading.

Born in a small Michigan town, the daughter of a local druggist, she owed her queer Christian name to the pungent, red berries which dot the moss-covered soil in the great pine-forests of that state. Her mother had always nourished a desire for these miniature fruits and, during the period of her daughter's gestation, she had cried out for them incessantly. In the last hours of her confinement she had screamed Wintergreen so lustily that it seemed predestined that the child should bear the name.

The mother had died in childbirth, and from that time on the father had neglected his profitable drug-business in order to indulge a secret conviction that he was a great inventor. Silas Waterbury's fantastic inventions—it will suffice to state that one of them was an extraordinary formula for metamorphosing grass into milk without the aid of a cow—came to nothing, and when the improvident druggist died, the heavy mortgages on such property as he apparently still possessed—he had borrowed money right and left to provide funds whereby he might carry out his preposterous schemes—were immediately foreclosed, and Wintergreen found herself penniless. Without any discernible ability—she had never even learned how to cook properly—the girl, nevertheless, had her dreams. She had watched with envy the rapidly ascending star of an old school-friend, Lottie Coulter, much less favoured in the matter of looks than Wintergreen herself. Only two years previously Lottie had gone on the stage in New York, and already she had acted two parts with the Provincetown Players, had been invited to become a member of the Actors' Equity Association, and had had her picture published twice in the New York Morning Telegraph. It was at Lottie's behest, with Lottie's encouragement, that Wintergreen determined that she, too, would go to New York. To accomplish this purpose, she wrote to Lottie for money, and received a cheque for seventy-five dollars by return mail.

The re-encounter of the two friends was a trifle strained. Wintergreen discovered that her old schoolmate had changed considerably. Her manner was more easy, her conversation—so sprinkled was it with the current argot of Broadway—well-nigh incomprehensible. Lottie, on her part, wondered exactly what she could do with the fresh, green country girl who stood before her. For the moment she could do nothing less than invite her to share her apartment. This apartment, on West Forty-ninth Street, offered abundant evidence of prosperity. Lottie explained to Wintergreen that she had furnished it with the profits of her two engagements with the Provincetown Players and, for the moment, until some of the greenness had worn away, Lottie considered it advisable to treat her old friend with circumspection, permitting her only such glimpses of her personal life as it seemed possible to surround with the requisite glamour of respectability. She need have made no exceptional effort in this direction. Wintergreen saw nothing irregular in the visits and conduct of the many young men who swarmed in and out of the place. For the rest, Lottie had warned them that they must keep their hands off the milkmaid.

For the moment, however, until she could be broken in, it was more convenient for Lottie to have Wintergreen out of the place a good part of the day, and she ransacked her brains and pestered her friends for a job for the druggist's daughter. It was difficult to arrive at a decision regarding the nature of this occupation, because, as has been stated, there was nothing that Wintergreen could do. Fortuitously, it was Wintergreen herself who solved the troublous problem. Thoroughly discouraged one day, she was a listless passenger on a Fifth Avenue bus. A man on the seat opposite her interrupted her confused reverie by accosting her politely and demanding if she were a model. At the moment she had not any very precise picture in her mind of what a model really was. The gentleman—she could see that he was a gentleman, because he was so polite—persisted in his attentions, inviting her to visit his studio, suggesting that he would offer her the customary stipend in exchange for the artistic use of her body. In desperation, she agreed to accept his proposition, not, however, without certain misgivings. To compensate for these she forced herself to consider her employment merely in the light of a makeshift, something to do until she might discover a more suitable profession. What this might be she had never previously been able to decide, but posing gave her an inspiration: she would become a painter.

From the beginning, she refused point-blank to pose nude, but her face was so pretty, so completely free from expressiveness of any kind, her features so even and unintelligent, that she made a superb model for the girl's head which plays so important a role on the cover of the American magazine, and soon she was in great demand. It cannot be denied that her beauty also won her other compliments. Artists, and brokers she met in their studios, besieged her with their unwelcome attentions, but one after another soon tired of the quest and dropped her, although she continued to give satisfaction in her professional capacity. They dropped her for the best of all reasons, because, apparently, she was impossible to possess.

Paul met her one afternoon at Jerry Trude's studio, whither he had repaired for cocktails. Struck at once by her dazzling appearance, he asked her to dine with him. Now, aside from her ruling passion, Wintergreen observed one other rule of conduct: she never refused food in whatever form it was offered. She had, therefore, been lunching or dining with Paul ever since, and had even consented to motor with him. She still, however, preserved her virginity, in every literal, physiological sense.

For Paul, her innate stupidity was part of her charm. It seemed to him that he had never before encountered any one who was stupid on so magnificent a scale. Even Amy and Vera would have lost the silver cup in any competition with this damsel. Paul held a theory about his peculiar taste for this sort of thing. He believed that he preferred to know women like Campaspe—was there, however, another?—as friends, but for a comfortable life with a wife or a mistress he invariably picked a moron.

One evening, after they had been acquainted for about a week, Paul determined to persuade this pretty lass to put herself to a more practical use on his account. He began the attack by ordering cocktails, doubles, moreover.

Wintergreen stared at him, wide-eyed, when the waiter set the brimming glasses before them.

You know I never drink, she expostulated.

Just one, tonight, he pleaded.

You wouldn't ask me to do that if you really respected me, she whimpered. It seemed probable that she was about to cry. Wintergreen had the instinct of tears. Where other women were compelled to act their grief, it came quite naturally to this simple child of Michigan. If any untoward incident occurred, especially anything directed at the validity of that vague condition which she was pleased to define as the respect due her from men, her eyes immediately were flooded. Pressed, she began to moan. If matters went further, she bawled. This was the protection the good God had given her for the virtue she held most dear. There was something about the spectacle of Wintergreen Waterbury in noisy sorrow which corroded the lust in strong men's hearts. Hardened roués had backed away from a demonstration of it in disgust; half-hearted swains turned and ran away from it for half-a-mile or so before they summoned enough courage to look over their shoulders. Paul was aware of this idiosyncrasy and of its habitual effect on others. It was obvious that it might easily cause the permanent destruction of his own desire, and so he did not press the point of cocktails.

I ordered them both for myself, dear, he explained.

Wintergreen's gloom lifted at once. She did not appear to have the faintest notion that alcohol in another person foreboded any danger to herself. It is doubtful, indeed, if she were aware when a man was drunk in her presence. Her stubborn theory in regard to liquor was limited to one axiom: drink, when consumed by young girls, invariably effected their downfall: Whether she had read this somewhere, or had been told, is not known. However that may be, she held the belief firmly.

Paul, who was patience itself when he had an object in view, did not relinquish the siege. On a later occasion he ordered champagne. This beverage, curiously enough, she imbibed willingly, apparently under the impression that it was a variety of ginger ale—Paul had selected a particularly sweet brand. Nevertheless, she still remained recalcitrant. There seemed to exist in her some blind, preservative instinct which continued to protect her, even after the small quantity of wine she had swallowed began to make its effect. She permitted Paul to hold her in his arms, to kiss her respectfully; she even went so far as to call him Dearie once or twice, but she baulked when he experimented tentatively in more significant directions. Their relationship resembled a game, which, indeed, so far as Paul was concerned, was as amusing as, possibly more amusing than, any consummation could possibly be. Apparently, in Wall Street, he was known as the possessor of a highly desirable mistress; in artistic circles, where the girl's reputation for the maintenance of strict behaviour was celebrated, it was supposed that he had been successful where all others had failed. Paul was aware of these misconceptions, and they added to the zest with which he pursued this unamorous phantom.

Wintergreen, on her side, was beginning to feel the need of a guide and confidante. So far, Lottie had not appealed to her as a sufficiently sympathetic listener, but there was no one else, and at last, one day, Wintergreen was inspired to recount to her some of the attentions Paul had paid her, concluding with, He's going to marry me.

Lottie, reclining on the bed, abruptly sat upright. Paul Moody! she exclaimed. Has he said so?

Why, no man would ever go so far with a girl as he has gone with me unless he wanted to marry her, would he? He loves me.

In your hat and over your ear! Has he said so?

Why, I kissed him!

You poor heel, you, was Lottie's comment. I don't know where you get 'em, if any.

Get what?

Brains, kid, brains. The tall blond can't marry you even if he wants to. He's married.

Married? Why didn't you tell me before? Wintergreen began to wail.

Well, for one thing, nitwit, because you only just this minute loosened up on his name.

But he'll divorce her to marry me!

Ha!

He will. You'll see! The girl was defiant. She had even stopped crying.

Has he said so?

No-o.

You poor, simple heel, you, how do you get that way? Somebody oughta crown you. Maybe that'd help.

Wintergreen began whimpering again. Why, what do you mean? she demanded.

I mean you gotta get wise. This ain't a boilermaker. These Wall Street johns can be trimmed.

Why, what do you mean? Wintergreen repeated.

Make him say something or do something.

I'm as pure as you are, Lottie Coulter! How dare you!

Snap it off, kid, snap it off. If you're as pure as I am you've got to go some. Don't you read the papers?

The papers? What papers? Wintergreen looked bewildered.

No papers, doll-baby, but the world knows the worst. My life's an open sewer.

Lottie!

I've reformed in a way, Lottie went on, rubbing the burning end of the stump of her cigarette against a plate which had held crackers, as she reflected that the hour for frankness had arrived. I've quit the hop for the junk.

The. . . ?

I've cut out lying on my hip and taken to inhaling the snow. . . Waving away the demand for further explanation she foresaw would be forthcoming, she hurried on, Well, let's leave that. Ancient history ain't any more important than the parsley on fish, but open your eyes, kid, open your eyes.

Wintergreen obeyed her literally.

We've got to get something on this guy, something juicy. Lottie lighted a new cigarette and puffed away thoughtfully. After a little, she continued, Then we'll have grounds for a breach of promise suit.

Wintergreen was incensed by this suggestion. He'll marry me, you'll see, she insisted.

May your children be acrobats! He'll marry Aunt Lottie sooner. But we'll prove that he wanted to marry you. To begin with you might scramble off that chaste lounge, and snatch a look at my pink taffeta. Do you know anything that'll take spots out? I spilled a whole dish of soup on it last night?

I've heard that ether. . .

Snap it off, kid. If I had any ether I'd drink it.

In the Moloch Club at this moment, Florizel Hammond, who had a fancy for old English ditties, was singing:

A rovin', a rovin',
For rovin's been my roo-i-n,
No more I'll go a rovin'
With you, fair maid!

Fourteen

In the days following Mrs. Pollanger's party, Campaspe fell prey to a mood which she uncharacteristically found impossible to shake off. She was thinking, more passionately than ever before, about herself, and her thoughts were black. Gunnar had leaped from the window to avoid her, of that there could be no reasonable doubt, and equally beyond question was the fact that this act bound her inextricably to him until they met again. His escape could not serve to free her; on the contrary, she was imprisoned by it. Looking back, she was reminded that it was the first time in her life she had experienced this unpleasant sensation. However that might be, she was experiencing it now—was no one ever secure, she was beginning to wonder?—and it was extremely disagreeable. She foresaw, indeed, a long period of revolting, and entirely uncustomary, perturbation ahead of her, unless she re-encountered Gunnar. And after? Well, whatever happened then, she readily admitted to herself, depended, precariously, on circumstances. She no longer felt any power within herself strong enough to protect her under certain conditions. With her brain she assured herself that she could still hold herself aloof from him, as she had succeeded, without any conscious effort, in holding herself aloof from other men, but her instinctive desire was so fervid that she did not know what she might do if she met him; she could not know. An unreasoning passion controlled her: her will was crumbling. At present, she was fully aware, she half-belonged to some one else, a state of affairs which she did not condone—rather, she loathed it—but over which, in the circumstances, she held no sway, nor could she anticipate any hope of recovery from this abhorrent emotional ailment save through a providential coincidence that would bring Gunnar before her eyes again. He had obviously run away. A man who would jump out of a window to evade a danger, at best only potential, was perfectly capable of jumping into a river or an ocean to conclusively end his panic. The simpler expedient of putting an ocean between him and the object of his fright might also have occurred to him. The consequence of the situation was that Campaspe hovered between a state of rude impatience and a feeling of impotence that possessed her with a tormenting rage. That her happiness should rest thus, even temporarily, in another's keeping was sufficient cause to infuriate her. She coveted then, with an eager ardour, this opportunity for one more meeting which—and on this point she was firmly determined—should ultimately settle the terms of their relationship.

In this hitherto unexperienced mood she derived her greatest solace through passing her time with Lalla Draycott. Lalla was as free from emotions, she took life as nonchalantly, as a grue in a French farce. Lalla's one interest centred in out-door sports. Every morning, accompanied by her bloodhound, Anubis, she rode in the park on a black stallion called Murder. At the proper seasons, in localities where the sport was possible and fashionable, she indulged in fox-hunting. She attended football and baseball games, and race-meets, and played golf and tennis. She knew the names of every celebrity mentioned in the sporting-pages of the newspapers. She could talk about Paavo Nurmi, Georges Carpentier, Jack Dempsey, Vincent Richards, or Epinard for an entire day without stopping, if any one would listen, whereas it is doubtful if she knew whether Anatole France was President of the Swiss Republic or a member of the Irish Parliament. She went to all the prize-fights and wrestling-matches in Madison Square Garden, usually occupying ringside seats. She enjoyed a bowing acquaintance with Tex Rickard. No horse-or dog-show ever opened without her presence. She wore mannish suits and smoked little cigars especially made for her.

Jack Draycott, thoroughly sympathetic with his wife's tastes, was her constant companion. Now, Campaspe had assumed the habit of going along too. She revived her long-forgotten custom of riding in the park. She again took up ice-skating, a smart diversion in New York this winter, at which she had once been an adept. The names of Gene Tunney, Abe Goldstein, Luis Angel Firpo, Tiger Flowers, Harry Wills, and Joe Lynch rolled easily off her tongue. She plunged whole-heartedly into this, to her, unfamiliar milieu in an effort the sooner to forget something she was finding it annoyingly difficult to forget. There was, however, another and even better reason for her avaricious adoption of the sporting life. She had the feeling that if she found Gunnar anywhere it would be in this environment. She never entered the ice-palace without anxiously scanning the faces of the instructors and the star-skaters. She never settled back to watch a prize-fight until she had assured herself that she was unacquainted with the features of the pugilists.

One morning—she had attended one of these bouts with Jack and Lalla the night before and gone out to supper afterwards—waking late, she was informed at once by Frederika that several pressing messages on the part of the Countess Nattatorrini had been delivered over the telephone. Campaspe immediately communicated with the Ritz. A strange voice explained that a nurse was speaking. The Countess was extremely ill; she had expressed a desire to see Mrs. Lorillard. Could she come at once? Mrs. Lorillard affirmed that she would be at the bedside as soon as she could dress, say in three-quarters of an hour.

Opening the door of the Countess's apartment at the appointed time, the nurse drew it nearly closed behind her and stepped out into the corridor.

I am so glad that you could come, Mrs. Lorillard, she began. The Countess is dying. The doctor, who has just gone, informs me that there is no hope. Last night she seemed better and we thought there might be a chance, but that faded away at dawn. The Countess is very much concerned because the priest has not arrived. I have telephoned for him twice, and was told, the second time, that he had not yet left the house. I thought if you would sit with her for a few moments I would go to fetch him. Her maid left several days ago, fearing infection. You know how cowardly French maids are. The Countess's malady is not infectious. There is nothing to do but just sit with her. Perhaps she may ask for something. Give her anything she wants. It doesn't matter now: nothing can hurt her any longer. She is conscious, but slightly delirious: she suffers from curious delusions. You will not, I hope, she concluded, gazing searchingly at Campaspe, find it too horrible.

Shaking her head, Campaspe quickly agreed to substitute for the nurse at the bedside of the dying woman, and as Miss Cottrell adjusted a blue cloak over her white uniform, Campaspe passed on through the salon into the sick-chamber. An overpowering scent harassed her nostrils, a nauseating confusion of some disinfectant with two floral odours which she detested. Clusters of white violets and stalks of tuberoses filled vases which stood on every available flat surface. The Countess, wasted by age and disease, lay on the bed. Her hair, usually so carefully arranged by the hairdresser, was combed straight back and bound loosely. Her eyes now stared unseeingly, now burned with a fierce and penetrating concentration on the object towards which they were directed. Her false teeth had been removed and, as a consequence, her cheeks were sunken hollows. When she saw Compaspe the old woman burst into tears. The nurse was right: it was horrible!

Why didn't you let me know that you were ill? Campaspe demanded.

I didn't want to bother you, Campaspe, the dying woman gasped. At first it was difficult to comprehend her, as her articulation was much affected by her lack of teeth. I didn't believe I was very sick, and I didn't want to bother you. . . One long, bony claw clutched convulsively at the bed-covering. . . Now I am no worse, no worse. . . Her voice rose to a shrill shriek which indicated that she would brook no denial. . . but I am so lonely, so lonely. . . She was whimpering. . . I want a priest, and where is my sister Lou?

Shall I send for her, Ella? Campaspe inquired.

Has no one sent for her, my sister Lou?

Seated before the desk, Campaspe removed a bowl of white violets, and sought a telegraph form. What is her address? she queried.

The Countess gave her this information, and while Campaspe indited the message, lay back gasping. After the boy had called to take it, she mumbled, May I have a glass of water, Campaspe? Where is Miss Cottrell?

She's gone on an errand. She'll be back directly. I'll get the water for you.

Why isn't she here? She should be here. I don't like to ask you to wait on me. The Countess was querulous.

Campaspe handed her the water. I'm only too glad to wait on you, dear Ella. I'll do anything you want done.

The bony claw continued to pluck the coverlet. A writhing shudder shook the skeleton lying under the bed-clothes. A hideous, glassy stare came into the eyes of the old woman, and she began to mutter, her lips gradually forming words, until, as she went on, eventually they gushed forth in a torrent. Wicked. . . Yes. . . Wicked. . . I have been. . . a very wicked. . . woman, Campaspe. Will God. . . Will God. . . forgive me, I wonder? How will he punish me? Yet, I meant. . . I meant it. . . to be all right. I was searching. . . searching. . . searching. I had a lantern, and they put it out. I lighted a candle and it was extinguished. They took it away from me. They took everything away from me. . . She sat upright. Campaspe, on the bed beside her, supported the poor, feeble frame. The Countess was for the moment, apparently, unaware of her presence. . . Cyril! she cried. You here! You've come back to me! You're sorry you left me? You won't go away again, will you? You'll stay with me now and make me happy! Tony, too! . . . Terror coloured the old woman's tones. . . You've all returned! she shrieked, trying to cover her face with her palms, but lacking the strength to lift her arms. All! Albert! Fernand! Gareth! Edgar! You're all here! Tell them to go away, Campaspe! Tell them to go away!

There, there, dear, be quiet. There's nobody here but me. Campaspe smoothed the sallow, fevered brow. The Countess, exhausted, sank back, her head once more cradled in the pillow. The tears flowed down her cheeks. I tried so hard to be happy, she sobbed. I wanted so much to be happy, only happy. I never did any one harm. But they all went away and left me alone. I cannot bear to be alone. Do you think God will forgive me for desiring just a little happiness?

I'm sure he will, dear. Campaspe continued to stroke the calid forehead.

My God, why have you made me suffer so much? Why have you denied me the happiness that others enjoy? Why have you made me a wanderer on the face of the earth, searching, for ever searching? Thy rod and thy staff did not comfort me. My cup was always empty. My days were numbered. . . Fierce anger dominated her now. . . I've had nothing, nothing. . . The bony claw convulsively clutched, clutched.

Her manner suddenly changed. Campaspe, she cajoled, open the drawer of that desk.

Campaspe obeyed her.

The photograph! The photograph! Her impatience was almost obscene.

In a Russian leather case Campaspe found the picture, taken in Nice, of a blond boy of radiant beauty, playing tennis. He reminded her of Hadrian's Bithynian Antinoüs, a classic Greek lad in white flannels.

Give it to me! Give it to me! the Countess screamed, snatching the case from Campaspe's proffering hand as soon as she could reach it.

Luigi! Luigi! she cried, kissing the photograph. I loved you! I love you still. How could you leave me, like all the others? Why were you, too, unfaithful to my dream? Did God take you away from me? I hate God! I hate God! I hate God!

Her words once more became an indistinguishable muttering; the photograph slipped from her fingers and lay, face downwards, on the coverlet. At last, the Countess was silent.

Presently, in a weaker voice, she inquired, Where is the priest?

He's coming in a moment, dear. Try to be patient.

I've been patient so long. I've waited and waited. I've not been so *very* wicked, after all, Campaspe. All I wanted was a little happiness, just once, that's all, just once. It was so little to ask, and yet God wouldn't give it to me. Will he forgive me, Campaspe? Where is the priest?

Coming, coming, dear.

Suddenly the expression in the senile, worn-out features altered. Weary lassitude gave way to a grisly leer. How do I know, she pondered aloud, but that this may be God's kindness? Perhaps he has held it in reserve until now. The priest is coming. Perhaps he. . .

The Countess, with her sunken cheeks, her staring eyes, the balls covered with a film, her clutching claws, was very terrible now. Campaspe grasped the arms of her chair tightly.

Campaspe, my teeth! I must have my teeth!

Campaspe discovered them in a tumbler of water on the ledge of the wash-basin in the bathroom. She carried the plates to the bedside.

My teeth! Campaspe, quick! The priest is coming. My teeth! My teeth!

Campaspe adjusted the plates in the vacant jaw.

My make-up, Campaspe! My lipstick! My rouge! My powder! Be quick! The priest is coming. Hasten!

Campaspe found the cosmetics in a dresser-drawer. Again she approached the bedside, but this time she faltered.

Make me up, Campaspe! Make me up! God is sending me a priest, a young, beautiful priest! Make me up!

Campaspe applied the rouge and powder to the wasted cheeks. She touched the brows and lashes with a blue pencil. She painted the lips a deep carmine.

My hair, Campaspe! My hair!

Campaspe combed the thin, white hair, and attempted to arrange it more becomingly.

Flowers, Campaspe! Strew the bed with flowers!

Campaspe cast stalks of fragrant tuberoses on the coverlet. Raising great clusters of white violets in her two hands, she scattered them on the bed.

My mirror! My mirror! With an amazing amount of energy, the Countess sat up again and regarded her reflection in the glass with obvious satisfaction. I am young again, she cried. Am I not young again, Campaspe?

You are marvellous, Campaspe assured her, but after one glance at the wreck before her, gruesome in this ghastly make-up, horrible in its wild expression of forlorn and ungratified lust, she turned her head away.

The outer door was heard to open. The aged woman gazed expectantly in the direction from which the caller must approach. The mirror she permitted to drop from her relaxed fingers to the floor, where it splintered into a thousand fragments.

The nurse entered, followed by the holy father. Even in dying, the Countess Ella Nattatorrini was doomed to disappointment. The priest was an old man.

Fifteen

The end of April found New York still cold and bleak. The buds on the trees were bursting and the birds were returning from the south because it seemed the proper season for these changes to take place, not because the buds and birds had received any encouragement from the elements. The sun refused to show his face for whole days and frosty winds blew chill rains up and down the streets. The result was that New Yorkers, who usually at this time of year began to suffer nostalgia for Europe or Maine, withdrew into their houses and huddled before active fireplaces, while they considered the advisability of another trip to Palm Beach or Havana.

To Campaspe, who seldom travelled in any direction, the weather was not a matter of any great moment. Her harassed state of mind was due to another cause. It seemed incredible to her that a man could destroy her habitual tranquillity, even temporarily, by leaping from a window, and yet it was patent that he had done so. There was, it would seem, sufficient diversion in the human scene to occupy her attention this spring, more, apparently, than usual, but every effort she made to direct her thoughts into more objective thoroughfares in some way or other led back to Gunnar. It was a good deal like taking a stroll in Venice: in whichever direction you sauntered, no matter how many corners you turned, or how careful you were to walk directly away from it, invariably, sooner or later, you turned up in the Piazza San Marco.

Paul, for instance, and his adventure in Wall Street, which had led him into the arms of a girl with the extraordinary name of Wintergreen Waterbury, obviously would repay investigation. Under ordinary circumstances Campaspe would have requested her friend to bring the model to tea so that she might examine her at closer range. Now she felt listless, uninterested, in the matter, save for her holding the curious, subconscious belief that it was through Gunnar that Paul had met Wintergreen. Gareth had reminded her that one pebble tossed into a still pool would create an ever-widening series of circles. Well, here the phenomenon was being enacted before her eyes. Other strange results of the maddening young man's peculiarly magnetic influence were to be noted in Consuelo's passion for instruction in the realm of acrobatics and in the successful launching of Miss Pinchon's amazing school. Of these, too, at the moment, it was impossible for Campaspe to reflect without pain. Only by a sort of double feat of mental ingenuity was she able to realize with what amusement she might regard this experiment on the part of the governess had it come about otherwise. In her present uncomfortably agitated mood she could derive no pleasure from a consideration of it, although it was obvious that contemplation of the project offered the most vital elements for cynical enjoyment. Pinchon's Prophylactic Plan, indeed, had assumed an international significance. Prospective pupils were arriving from Europe, Indiana, and California by every ship and train, each nourishing the practical intention of winning a diploma by means of which they might carry the secrets of the Plan into their own particular camps. A very celebrated philosophical writer had manifested his interest in the institution by introducing encomiastic references to it in his lectures. It was rumoured that Havelock Ellis had written a letter of query in regard to it. In the pleasant breeze created by this spreading fan of recognition Miss Pinchon had been obliged to provide larger quarters and to engage new professors both for the philosophical and physical departments. George Everest, it appeared, would probably earn large dividends from his initial investment of one thousand dollars.

One afternoon, returning from a drive to Great Neck with Lalla, who had gone out with the purpose of inspecting some English sheep-dogs in a kennel there, Campaspe, seated before the fireplace in her drawing-room, considered these matters. She had not changed her dress since she had come in and still wore a dark-green velvet suit, cut in a severe tailored fashion, with a small, moss-coloured straw cloche, devoid of ornament. Attempting to apply her mind to the inspection of these topics which would have interested her so much at any other time, it seemed to her that the logs in the fire were assuming the attitudes of acrobats about to undertake some difficult feat. In her imagination the andirons metamorphosed themselves into the supporting bases for a taut wire, and the clock on the mantelpiece ticked, without cessation, Gun-nar! Gun-nar! Gun-nar!

With a great effort of the will she induced her mind to consider another incident, that of the death of Ella Nattatorrini. How difficult it had proved to invent, without preparation, a history which might be retailed safely to Lou Poore! She had in no adequate manner sensed in advance what this sister would be like; somehow she hadn't thought about it at all, but when she saw the poor, simple, frail, old lady standing before her, she was cognizant at once of the fact that this was the kind of person who must be regaled with a suitably sympathetic deathbed story. Campaspe had risen magnificently to the occasion, had described the Countess calling to have the windows opened so that she might believe she were in Iowa once more, had recounted how, propped up against the pillows, Ella had imagined she stood once again in the fields of waving corn; then, how she had uttered her father's name twice, and had asked for her sister just before she expired. The poor old lady had thanked her, weeping softly, and had departed happy, or as happy as any one could be made by a deathbed story. Campaspe wondered, indeed, if the death of the Countess under these glamorous conditions were not calculated to make Lou happier even than she had been while her sister lived. Lou must always instinctively have resented the living Ella. Sympathetically, as well as geographically, they must have dwelt thousands of leagues apart. It was only in death, as a matter of fact, that Lou possessed Ella once more as a sister. Now, probably, she would create for herself a legend of a great love. The real scene, what had actually occurred, on the other hand, belonged to Campaspe alone, and was inextricably complicated and confused in her mind with the thought of her own great desire.

She lifted another log from the copper sugar-kettle which held the supply and laid it on the fire almost reverently, as though she were offering a sacrifice to the gods. Outside, she was aware, the clouds were breaking and the drizzle had ceased. The creaking and rattling of the casements, however, gave evidence that a high wind was blowing.

The clock in the process of striking five was interrupted by the faint, far-away tinkle of the doorbell. Presently, Campaspe heard Frederika softly making her way along the hallway towards the street entrance. She did not wish to see anybody, but her lassitude was so complete that she lacked the force to warn Frederika that she was not at home. She remained, therefore, quietly gazing into the fire, as she listened to the opening and closing of the door. Now she sensed a presence in the room, but even so she did not yet turn her head. There followed a considerable pause before her visitor spoke.

I have come back, she heard a breaking voice announce.

Still she did not turn her head. How thankful she was that she had not turned it before! She waited, perhaps ten seconds, employing all the will at her command in a supreme effort to regain her composure. Then she spoke—and how hollow and unreal her voice sounded to her!

Yes. How do you do? At last, she risked a glance. How pitiful he was, with agony sketched across his features! The glance performed the miracle she had been praying for. She might have known that she could count on that. Confronted by his distress, her own peace of mind returned in some degree. She even rose, advanced towards him, and clasped his hand.

Please. . . sit down, she invited.

He did not accept her invitation. He remained standing; he was not, she observed, even looking in her direction.

I have fought like ten million devils, he stammered, but it's no good. I love you. He made this announcement in a tone of the deepest despair.

I think I love you, too, Gunnar, Campaspe responded. Then she celebrated an astonishing ceremony. Pressing his temples between her palms, she kissed him on the forehead. Cluttering into an arm-chair, the young man held his hands before his eyes and wept.

I think, Campaspe continued, softly, that you will have a good deal to tell me. . . With her hand she touched him gently on the shoulder, but she did not try to comfort him with words. . . This is scarcely the place. At this hour we may be interrupted. Later I have people coming to dinner. If you don't mind we'll go out.

Gunnar nodded a weary acquiescence. Campaspe rang.

Frederika, she ordered, telephone Ambrose to bring the car around immediately. Mr. and Mrs. Draycott and Mr. Hammond are coming to dine at eight. If I have not returned, ask them to sit down without me. Explain to them that I have been detained.

Yes, madame. What dress shall I lay out?

It doesn't matter. Campaspe was impatient. Then an inspiration came to her. The silver, Frederika, she said.

Heavy, purple clouds again masked the sky and shut the light from the New York streets. The room was in almost total darkness save for the glow from the fire. The two sat in absolute silence. Not a word was spoken, not a glance exchanged, during the ten minutes they waited for the car. When, at last, Ambrose was announced, Campaspe said quietly, Come, and Gunnar rose and followed her.

She whispered a direction to the chauffeur before she settled back into her seat. As Ambrose started the car, she peered at Gunnar. His face, still preserving somehow that inexplicable effulgent aureole which seemed mystically to illuminate his countenance, wore, she thought, the most utterly despondent expression she had ever observed on human features. And quite suddenly, she began to breathe naturally again, aware that by some magic accident she was released, free once more, at any rate her own, and no one else's, able to deal with the situation, with any situation, able again to lead her own special, personal life. On and on they drove in the closed car, Ambrose directing it straight ahead towards their mysterious destination. Now and again, she patted Gunnar's hand, but still no word was spoken. Presently, the purple clouds burst and whips of rain lashed the windows. At last, on a side street off Riverside Drive, the automobile drew up before a frame house of modest size, set back some distance on a broad lawn. Ambrose raised an umbrella to protect the pair from the downpour as he escorted them through the gate up the walk to the house. On the porch, Campaspe inserted a key in the lock, opened the door, and led Gunnar into a dark hallway. Pressing a button she caused a red globe, which depended on a chain from the ceiling, to glow with light. The pair ascended the stairs. On the second storey she took a turn down the corridor, passing several closed doors, until she selected one which she opened. Again she pressed a button.

They stood in a bedroom, furnished neatly, simply. The wall-paper was the shade of ivory, spattered symmetrically with sprigs of blue flowers. Curtains of dotted swiss hung before the windows. The bed, covered with a white counterpane, embroidered in blue and rose, the reniform dresser, laid out with all necessary toilet articles, the chest of drawers, and the chairs were all of birds'-eye maple.

Sit down, Gunnar, Campaspe urged.

He accepted a chair. There was another formidable pause. Campaspe had seated herself on the bed, leaning back against the headboard. She extracted a cigarette from her case and struck a match.

Now, she said, exhaling a whiff of smoke of the hue of the moonstone, tell me why you have come back, and why you went away.

You know the answer to both those questions, Gunnar replied.

It would be better, perhaps, if you began at the beginning, Campaspe suggested.

Gunnar supported his head in his interlocked hands against the back of his chair. Once more Campaspe sensed an eerie impression of a halo. After he began to speak she scarcely once removed her direct gaze from his face. Gunnar's eyes, on the contrary, shifted away from this close scrutiny. At first, his speech was halting and low, but as his feeling for his narrative grew warmer, he spoke faster and louder.

Well then, he said, I must begin before I was born. My father, John Aloysius O'Grady is an Irishman and a most remarkable man. He married Beata Fuchs, an Austrian Jewess, who is an equally remarkable woman. Neither relinquished their religion. My father has remained a Catholic to this day, and my mother continues to observe the faith of her race in the synagogue. Singularly enough, in the face of this friendly disagreement in regard to their religious beliefs, they were able to agree on a much more difficult question, the rearing of their offspring.

My father had long since made the acute observation that whether children were brought up strictly or leniently by their parents the gods were ironically indifferent. One boy, prepared for all the pitfalls of life, fell into all the snares and traps he had been so carefully warned to avoid; another boy, reared in precisely the same manner, heeded the warning. Or, in the opposite instance, a lad, whose parents neglected to acquaint him with any of the perils of life, somehow managed, quite unconsciously, to walk around the danger spots and remain innocent until the day he died, while another, with an exactly similar background, spent his youth with loose women, drank to excess, dabbled in drugs, and at fifty suddenly collapsed in the street and was carried off to a hospital. Life, indeed, certainly so far as the raising of children was concerned, appeared to be a vicious circle. My father passed a good many of his early years in communion with the philosophers, a pernicious habit in which, two decades later, I futilely followed him. They taught him nothing. At the end of this period, however, through a long process of reasoning which I shall not detail to you, he became convinced that parents, through the very personal nature of their interest, were entirely unfitted to bring up their own children. Shortly after he had arrived at this radical conclusion he invented his extraordinary plan which offered the further advantage of removing any possibility of argument in regard to the religious faith in which his children were to be reared. When the plan was broached to my mother she immediately consented to its adoption. This agreement was reached when my eldest sister Dagmar was two years old.

Three years later, when Dagmar was five, an age at which she could walk and talk and think and was about to begin her quest of worldly knowledge, my father gave her in charge to a sterile couple who had long desired to possess a child. These foster-parents were only selected after a great deal of preliminary study—many excellent offers were rejected. The investigations, however, were conducted through the medium of a third person. An ineluctable rule of my father's system stipulated that foster-parents and actual parents should never meet. A clause was inserted, however, to the effect that the contract should come to an end when Dagmar attained her twenty-first year, that is, she should then be informed of the state of affairs and should choose for herself whether to live with one or the other couple, or both, at intervals, or neither. This plan was followed in every detail, without variation, with four more children.

Five years ago, when I reached my majority, I was invited to join my parents and learn the facts that I have just related to you in abbreviated form. My sister Dagmar, now one of the foremost scientists of Germany—you doubtless are acquainted with her book dealing with the spiritual identity of the circle and the square—learned them two years before me. As for my brothers and sisters who still remain in ignorance of their paternity, it may be said that they, too, have already in a measure justified the experiment. Cécile has made her début as a violinist and her hand has been sought in marriage by a French gentleman of the highest social standing. Giuseppe is one of the leaders of the Fascisti—you may have observed his name in the papers. As for Zimbule. . .

Zimbule! Campaspe echoed, stupefied. Zimbule O'Grady!

Yes, the actress whom the New York dramatic critics have recognized as this season's American Duse.

But how strange all your Christian names are! And by what method have you contrived to hold on to the O'Grady?

Gunnar leaned so far back into his chair that his long eyelashes formed shadows on his eyeballs, like the patterns made on white sand by palm-leaves in the sun. That is extremely simple, he continued. An essential clause in the contract stipulated that we should retain our surname, and to avoid discussion as to whether we should receive Irish or Jewish Christian names it was further nominated that we should only be given these upon the occasion of our pseudo-adoption. We were then christened by our foster-parents, and the diversity in our names is accounted for by the fact that my father and mother, who are immensely wealthy, travelled extensively, a condition which was facilitated by their absolute freedom from all family responsibility.

Zimbule was given in charge to a Levantine family. She has undergone a curious experience, but even in the face of a bewildering series of accidents my father's faith in his plan has been justified. Shortly after she had been adopted by this worthy Levantine couple, they departed on a voyage for America. The steamship in which they embarked was wrecked off the coast of Newfoundland. They, together with nearly every other soul aboard, perished. By some kind of miracle, however, Zimbule was saved. What happened to her subsequently is as yet a mystery. My parents only heard of her again when she became a moving-picture star. Doubtless, on the occasion of her reunion with her lost ones, which will occur in a few years, she will be able to relate the incidents, of the unaccounted-for period in her career.

But the name! Campaspe cried. How has she been able to retain the name?

Easily, Gunnar explained. Each of us, at the time of our adoption and christening, was presented with a gold key on which the name was engraved. This key was attached to a gold chain linked around the throat and could only be removed by breaking the chain. The key opens a box kept by our guardians in a safe-deposit vault, waiting our coming of age. Zimbule's box was secured by my parents after her foster-family had perished at sea. She doubtless retains the key.

I saw no key! Campaspe exclaimed.

Do you then know her? Gunnar regarded her with astonishment.

I knew her two years ago.

Even if she does not wear it round her throat, she must have retained the key, Gunnar argued.

It is a most amazing story, Campaspe commented, as she lighted a new cigarette.

There is much more, and the interesting part of it is that it is all true, but I must come down to my own history, making it as brief as possible.

You need not abbreviate it on my account, Campaspe urged. I am willing to listen two days or longer.

I was brought up by a Danish family in Copenhagen, Gunnar continued; hence my name, Gunnar. My guardian was an honest burgess of some fortune; his wife, a sedate and careful housewife. The incidents of my childhood are not essential to this narrative and I shall not go into them. Suffice it to say that I was sent to the University at Copenhagen, famous, as you may have heard, for its training of athletes, and it was there that I became proficient in the Grecian games.

I always nourished an instinctive desire to develop my body. My ambition was to force my muscles to be subservient to my slightest whim. Perfect coordination was my aim. As I grew older and became more interested in the philosophy of life, an inclination inherited, probably, from my father, this instinct seemed even more reasonable to me. I looked about, and what did I see? People, consumed with hate and rage and lust, existing like squirrels in their cages, continuously and unnecessarily pawing perdurable treadmills. For what? Only to cause them to revolve. Others reminded me more of panthers in the zoological gardens, striding incessantly behind their bars from one side of the enclosure to the other. I began to think of my fellow-beings as mechanical toys, automatically performing the rites of coeval or geographical morality or custom, with occasional baffling and disturbing interruptions caused by the fierce demands of sex or greed. There appeared to be no justification for life, no sense to it. I foresaw that I should become like the others. It was during this fatal period that I came upon the studies of Sigmund Freud and, convinced as I was at the time that there was truth in his diagnosis of the universal neurosis, I was quite prepared to commit suicide.

What I actually did do. . . Gunnar now looked Campaspe full in the eyes. . . was something much worse. I fell in love. Here, too, I shall abridge, giving you only the essentials of an affair to which I might easily devote ten evenings, or write down in a book which would be longer than à la Recherche du temps perdu. I fell in love with a lady who apparently loved me also. It was arranged, after a short but seething courtship, that we should be married. One evening, however, shortly before that solemn ceremony was to be celebrated, she persuaded me to yield to her charms, and our physical union was consummated. The events of the next two months assumed the form of a hideous vision—even yet there seems nothing real to me in this sordid adventure. I was completely in the power of lust. There was, assuredly, no happiness in those months; rather, every variety of misery and grief and anguish and humiliation, together with the fierce, nervous excitement brought about by the abuse of our natural forces. Jealousy, devastating, burning, consuming jealousy, devoured my vitals. I was jealous even of the motor that bore her to our rendezvous, jealous of the hours that kept her away from me, jealous of the servants to whom she gave orders. When I was perforce separated from her for a day I cursed her and myself. I was unable to work. I was unable to enjoy myself. In short, he concluded, his lip curling bitterly, I was in love.

You were, indeed, Campaspe echoed sympathetically.

Love, I found, is not happiness. It is a kind of consuming selfishness which ends in slavery. You belong to some one else. You no longer live with yourself. You lose your freedom and become the servant of glowering moods and the powers of darkness. You suggest a shadow rather than an object. The orientals, I understand, take these matters more lightly—Sigmund Freud would find no patients among the

Arabs—but with us Northern races love is the bane of our existence. He paused to mop his face with his handkerchief. I shall not try your patience much longer, he announced.

Go on! Go on! Campaspe urged. Say all that you have to say!

I am nearly done. Day by day, I found myself growing weaker, readier to answer the call of the loathsome voice, and more stricken with the bitter, reactionary pain which has no surcease until, at last, I struck bottom. I discovered that my mistress, my affianced bride, was unfaithful to me, unfaithful in a manner with which, through a curious chain of circumstances, I became fully cognizant. At first, I planned to kill her. For days, indeed, I was mad, completely, totally insane. Quite suddenly, my brain, or my body—can one ever be sure which it is?—experienced an unexpected but salutary revulsion. I would, I determined, kill this thing in *me,* instead, and be free again. At that instant my drooping spirits began to revive.

There were, however, other dangers to guard against. There was the possibility that I might fall into step with the automatic puppets, become one of the squirrels in the treadmill, or one of the restless panthers behind the bars. In whichever direction I turned life seemed to be hopelessly dominated by these conditions: stupid, ovine existence, complicated, and often rendered ridiculous, by the arduous rigours of sex. The married were not free from it, less free from it, indeed, than the unmarried. With married couples I noted a constant suggestion of straining on the leash, a desire to break away into forbidden fields. Some, of course, did break away to console themselves with libidinous debauchery, which they tried to construe as comfort or happiness. In any event, the strain was always intense, mutual hatred under the surface at times, but always ready, in case of accident, to rear its ugly head.

I desired complete freedom. What was there to do in life? Conform to the action of the puppets, dull one's perceptions and lead the existence of the majority, an existence which appeared to me to have no meaning, or. . . ? I sought advice from the philosophers. I began to read Plato and Pythagoras, Plotinus, Kant, Schopenhauer, Nietzsche. . . even Hans Vaihinger, but it was not until I stumbled upon Hippias, the old Greek, that I discovered any food to satisfy my natural craving. Have you ever heard of Hippias?

Campaspe shook her head.

Well, the philosophy of Hippias embraced all of life. He believed that one should cultivate everything inside oneself. He himself was an extraordinary mathematician; he practised poetry and he understood astronomy. Painting, mythology, ethnology, as well as music, held his interest. He designed and made his own garments; he fashioned his own jewelry. He also appears to have held an ideal looking forward to the establishment of a universal brotherhood, an obnoxious ideal which I did not take over. . . There was also at hand the case of Leonardo da Vinci. . .

Of him I know.

Naturally. Well, Hippias was my salvation. I knew at last what I might do: I might strive for perfection, so far as was humanly possible. Already a fine athlete, I determined to make my body the most agile in the world. Heard I of a feat attempted by another I accomplished it too. I was already acquainted with many languages. I had waded through all the philosophies. Lately, I have mastered the art of humility, together with an enormous amount of prowess in the field of salesmanship, by engaging in small clerkships and certain of the so-called inferior trades. Also I have acquired enough technical experience of a social nature so that I manage to get along fairly well with the puppets. I was well on my way towards my goal of perfection. I was light-hearted, carving out a form of existence which might have proved an irresistible model to other young men, when. . . I met you. Now I have lost my freedom again. Once more I am plunged in misery, suffer with cold sweats, endure the sense of fear that masters a man no longer master of himself. In short I am experiencing anew all the awful agony of love. I tried escape. I sought to run away. Gunnar groaned. It was impossible. I felt drawn back involuntarily. I cannot get along without you and yet my reason tells me that I am miserable every instant I am with you. What am I to do?

I suppose, Campaspe replied, as if she were reflecting, that the flaw in your system—and every system of philosophy must have at least a single flaw—is that you have overlooked the importance of preparing for the reactions of the sex impulse.

It must be stamped out, he cried.

That is exactly what you cannot do. You are finding out that no life is possible which excludes sex. I know. I, too, have suffered. During the weeks you have been away I have felt a good deal—not so much, perhaps, because it didn't frighten me so much—of what you must have been feeling. I, too, for a somewhat different reason, desire to be free, and it needed just this to set me free. I have seen you now, talked with you, kissed you, and I have escaped from my desire, because I have given it up of my own accord. Had you kept away from me I could never—

well, certainly not for a long time—have liberated myself, because I would not have been exercising my own free will. Your absence would have been a compelling factor which would have acted unfavourably.

And I? he demanded bitterly. What about me?

Campaspe rose, stooped over Gunnar, and grasped his shoulders. Why, she queried, do you think I brought you here?

Why? he echoed, stupefied. Why?

Here I am. Here you are. There is the bed. I am strong enough now to give you what you want and still walk away free. I am willing to do so. . . She was speaking with great gentleness. . . If you want to be free also you must reject me of your own accord, with your own will. Are *you* strong enough?

As she removed her hands from his shoulders, Gunnar bowed his head into his palms and wept.

Gunnar, Gunnar, I am so sorry, so very sorry. Campaspe tried to console him.

Can't you see how unfair you are? he inquired at last. You are only giving your strength to my weakness, which binds me to you ten times more tightly. I could only escape if you wanted me as much as I want you. Then I might use my will. Now, it is you who have rejected me. You are offering me a shell to play with, a shell which would enclose and bind me to you, while you are bound to nothing.

That, Campaspe averred sadly, I cannot help. I can give you no more than I can give you. I am compelled to tell you the truth: I am free.

Then, he said, rising, there remains but one thing for me to do.

She did not try to comfort him further. She knew the vanity of any such attempt. As she led him stumbling from the house, it appeared to her that the amber glow about his brow flickered uncertainly. Suddenly, without a word of farewell, he dashed away down the rain-swept street.

At a quarter before eight, Frederika was fastening the hooks on Campaspe's silver gown. Campaspe, polishing her nails, glanced occasionally into a long mirror to note the effect of her costume.

Be sure, Frederika, she was saying, that there is enough ice in the Bacardi cocktails, and less grenadine than last time.

Yes, Mrs. Lorillard.

And I do hope cook hasn't forgotten to put garlic in the lamb.

No, madame.

If Campaspe harboured any other qualms about the dinner she forgot them. A line from Edith Dale's letter had slipped into her mind, the line descriptive of the horror in the chapel of the Penitentes: whitewashed walls. . . splotched with blood-splashing. . . a little wagon with wooden wheels on which was seated a life-sized skeleton, laughing, bearing bow and arrow, the arrow poised, the bow drawn. . . She heard the bell below ring faintly. Presently, the door was opened, and Lalla Draycott's hearty voice reverberated through the corridor.

Sixteen

The situation regarding Wintergreen Waterbury, unchanged and unchanging, was beginning to try Paul's patience. Long since, he had lost all interest in everything pertaining to the affair save the sporting chance. It was disagreeable to his pride to be forced to admit that he had failed where all others had failed. The girl's placid virginity was baffling. Apparently, she made no slightest effort to protect her most cherished possession: she accepted all invitations with alacrity, lunched, dined, motored, and supped with Paul with a casual docility that, in another case, would have offered evidence of interest. When the atmosphere became unpleasantly warm she wept. On one occasion she had cried continuously for nearly an hour. After ten minutes or so of this startling exhibition he had felt impelled to time this test of endurance. Lately, she had been given to dropping mysterious hints. With any one else, or had there been anything in their relationship to provoke such a thought, he would have believed that she was enticing him to propose marriage to her. With Wintergreen, however, the idea was incredible, preposterous. Still there was something going on in what took the place of her mind; of that there could be no doubt.

Had there been anything to gain in the end beyond a certain sop to his vanity, Paul perhaps might have continued the pursuit of conquest for six months or even a year. As it was, he felt bored and it required some strength of mind on his part to continue the hunt for even a week longer. At last, he determined, with grim irony, to set a time limit to his sport. If, he decided, I can get no further in ten days, I shall send her back to her studios as chaste as she was when I met her.

The last day of this period fell on the fifteenth of May, and the fifteenth of May was at hand. For this final siege Paul had arranged a luncheon at an unfrequented roadhouse off the main thoroughfare, but in the general direction of Yonkers. On any occasion it was impossible to persuade this nymph of Diana to eat in a private room, but in this particular roadhouse it was fairly certain that the main dining-room would be unoccupied at midday.

He called for Wintergreen at a little after twelve and kicked his heels restlessly in Lottie's sitting-room. It is the custom of Chinese mandarins to keep distinguished visitors waiting for an hour to show them that they are doing them the honour of preparing for the call. Wintergreen was not consciously acquainted with this code of behaviour, but her temperament precluded the possibility of her ever meeting any engagement at the time appointed. When, at last, she joined him, Paul felt that he had never before seen her appear quite so beautiful. Her straight, black hair was bound back on her head under a grape-blue cloche and her body was enclosed in a frock of cardinal crepe de chine. Her face was pale, her lips crimson, and a curious confusion of innocence and suspicion peeped out from under her long lashes.

Never amusing, except when she talked about her future career as a painter, on this afternoon Wintergreen proved to be particularly dull. Her first question, as always, was Where are we going? Once in the motor, she displayed her usual interest in the road, most of which she had traversed with Paul twenty times before. How often she had requested him to tell her the name of the beautiful drive along the river bank, and how often he had told her! She invented a new query for this occasion, demanding information as to the exact point at which the Hudson met the North River. Once or twice, Paul attempted to clasp her hand in his palm. The first time this occurred she withdrew her hand shyly, even a little coyly, he was inclined to believe. He was led to make further effort in this direction.

I don't believe you think I'm nice, she protested.

Wintergreen—how he loved to utter that name; aside from her invulnerable chastity, it was the best excuse for his fancy for the girl—indeed, I do. I think you're very nice.

If you thought I was nice, you wouldn't do that, unless. . .

Unless what?

Nothing, she responded, turning her head away to gaze at a great castle that reared its towers on the rocks above the road.

How fast can this car go? was her next question.

I don't know, he replied carelessly. I suppose sixty or seventy miles an hour.

O! Are we driving that fast now?

We'd be arrested for speeding if we were.

How fast are we driving?

I suppose about twenty miles. Paul yawned. He made a mental vow never to undertake the seduction of another moron.

O, is that all? Tell him to drive sixty miles.

Do you want to spend the night in jail?

Why, Paul, how can you ask me such a thing? I don't believe you think I'm nice.

A suspicious tremor in her voice alarmed her escort.

Wintergreen, he explained hastily, there are laws against speeding. If we drove faster we might be arrested. That is all I meant.

Wintergreen was pacified, but not convinced. She appeared to be deliberating.

Who would arrest us? she demanded, after a pause.

Policemen are stationed along the road for that purpose.

She looked about her. I don't see any policemen, she announced, incredulous.

You never can tell where they will be.

I don't remember that we've passed any.

Sometimes they hide behind the walls.

It was evident, this time, that the girl thought he was lying to her. You don't think I'm nice or you wouldn't say that! she whimpered.

In desperation Paul appealed to the chauffeur.

Sam, have you seen any cops?

You can't spot 'em on this road, sir. They hide. But we ain't goin' fast enough to matter. Barely ten miles.

This corroboration had a brightening effect on Wintergreen. I really didn't believe, Paul, she averred, that you would treat me like a bad girl.

As Paul had foreseen, the inn was practically deserted. To be sure, the dining-room already held one occupant, but he was assuredly too drunk to be observant. His head and arms sprawled on the table before him. A high-ball glass had been overturned and the table was wet with its contents, which still dripped to the floor. Paul gave one glance at this dilapidated figure and then forgot about it.

A phonograph in one corner of the room, fortified with a repeater and an electric attachment, was negotiating without respite a curious, languid strain, sung by a Negress:

Michigan Waters ain't like cherry wine;
I said cherry,
I mean wine.
Michigan Waters ain't like cherry wine;
I'm gwine back to Michigan to the one I left behine.

What a silly song, Wintergreen commented. Of course, Michigan water isn't like cherry wine. It isn't, she asserted, with an air of authority—had not she herself been born in Michigan?—like any kind of wine at all. It's like water, just like water anywhere; just like, she went on, in an attempt to explain her meaning more fully, the water in the Hudson River, or the water we drink. And who ever heard of a Nigger wanting to go back to Michigan?

On this last day of the siege Paul made one final attempt to ply the girl with liquor, but she was more than usually well provided with refusals. He thought of another way to please her: he would flatter her by inviting her to order the luncheon. He had cause to regret this rash act. She began by asking for alligator pears stuffed with crab-meat and bathed in mayonnaise. A filet mignon, flanked by side dishes of lima beans, green peas, and French fried potatoes, was to follow. She chose chocolate ice-cream on apple-pie to conclude this repast. As she raised no objection to Paul's drinking, he ordered a cocktail.

I ate so much hot rabbit that I hopped just like a kangaroo;
I said kanga—
I mean roo—
I ate so much hot rabbit that I hopped just like a kangaroo; Daddy, if you ain't got nobody, let me hop for you.

I just love food, Wintergreen confessed.

It's good for you, little girl, he advised her. You're growing, and you need it.

Suspicious that he was spoofing her, she gave him a sullen glance, and only the arrival of the alligator pear averted an unpleasant scene.

There's two kinds o' people in this world that I can't stan';
I mean that I can't stan';
There's two kinds o' people in this world that I can't stan';
That's a two-faceted woman and a monkey man.

Not vitally interested in the pear, finding his cocktail a little acid, bored with the situation in general, reflecting that in the rôle of Casanova he appeared to be a failure, Paul's gaze wandered round the room. Across the waste of unoccupied tables he noted that the drunken fellow had not altered his position. Curious that the waiters had made no attempt to remove him. Paul's eyes strayed on until they caught the windows, and through one of these they beheld a petrifying vision.

From the limbs of a crab-apple-tree in full bloom, a child, in gymnasium bloomers, hung by her calves, in such a position that she could see directly into the room. What appeared to be still more astonishing was the fact that her eyes were focused on the limp figure in the corner. An inexplicable instinct informed Paul that he was acquainted with the rural trapezist, but it was difficult to identify the features of the reversed face. His more serious scrutiny was rewarded: he recognized Consuelo!

He glanced across the table at Wintergreen. She was engaged in devouring her alligator pear in a manner suggesting that she had not tasted food for days. Don't you want mine too? he urged. I'm not hungry.

Mouth full, she assented with an Um.

Will you excuse me for a moment while I telephone?

She gave permission with another Um.

Paul hastened from the room, down the stairs, out of the door into the yard. He crept stealthily around the side of the house. Before him now, the pink blossoms of the crab-apple-trees, set on a green embankment, hugged the blue of the sky. Consuelo had abandoned her striking posture and was sitting on the bough, while a prim, elderly woman below was imploring her to descend.

Consuelo, please, please, come down!

I won't. Not yet.

If you don't come down at once I shall be obliged to telephone your mother.

I don't care. She can't get here for another hour.

I'll fetch a ladder, the woman threatened.

Miss Graves, if you do that I'll climb to the topmost branch and leap to another tree.

Nimbly, like a monkey, to exhibit her prowess, she made her way from limb to limb. Pink petals in showers fluttered to the verdant sward. The governess wrung her hands and wept. What shall I do? she moaned. What shall I do? What a child!

At this moment Consuelo caught sight of Paul.

Why, Mr. Moody, she cried, what in the world are you doing here?

I might ask you the same question, he replied. Please come down and tell me.

Friend or enemy?

Friend.

I'll come down. Projecting her body towards the trunk of the tree she slid earthwards.

Now! Paul demanded.

Now! Consuelo echoed. Very well. I've no secrets. Gunnar returned to the gymnasium today—I always knew he would—and when he left, I followed him.

I couldn't persuade her not to, Miss Graves whined. The best I could do was to accompany her. I'll lose my position without a reference.

Paul was not listening to the governess's explanation. Followed Gunnar? he queried, mystified. Then, where is he?

In there! Consuelo announced, pointing towards the window.

In there! Why there's nobody in there!

Yes, he is, with his head on the table.

That can't be Gunnar. That fellow's drunk.

Gunnar is drunk, she affirmed positively. He was drunk when he came to the gymnasium. That's why I couldn't talk to him there! That's why I can't talk to him now!

Well, what do you propose to do?

It's enough to be near him, but I think I'll stay here until he is sober.

You might have to wait a week.

I know, and Miss Graves is so impatient. Can't you persuade her to be sensible?

Paul, on reflection, came to the conclusion that this task might prove difficult. I'll tell you what I'll do, he said. I'll go inside and talk to him.

That's a splendid suggestion, Consuelo agreed, and I'll go with you.

Paul remembered Wintergreen. No, Consuelo, he protested, that won't do. You say yourself that he's intoxicated. Did you bring a car?

Pointing to a taxi, parked in the automobile shed, Consuelo said, That's mine.

Jump in then, and wait until I see what can be done.

You promise to come back?

Of course, I'll come back.

After escorting the child and her governess to the car, Paul made his way back into the house and up the stairs to the dining-room. His first thought was of Wintergreen. He must appease her after his long absence. Sighting her table, a new miracle met his eye: Wintergreen with a cocktail before her and with Gunnar's right arm around her shoulders. They chose this precise moment to kiss.

I'll be damned! cried Paul.

The pair looked up. An expression of annoyance crossed the girl's countenance.

You leave us alone! she growled.

Ignoring her protestation, Paul cried, Gunnar, I'm delighted to find you again!

Who're you? O'Grady shot out thickly. O, Moody. Well, get out!

Paul, puzzled, persisted. Why, Gunnar, what's the matter?

You heard him, Wintergreen affirmed grimly.

Paul could not resist this opening. I thought, he commented, that you were a nice girl!

Dare call her anything else!

Turning to Gunnar, Wintergreen presented him first with her admiring glance, then with her lips.

Well, I'll be damned! Paul exclaimed once more. Was there, reasonably, any alternative comment?

Let's get out of this! Gunnar urged. Let's get a private room. Waiter, he called, we want a room upstairs where we won't be interrupted.

Certainly, Mr. O'Grady.

And bring up some wine! he called over his shoulder as, with Wintergreen on his arm, he staggered out of the restaurant.

I believe to my soul my man's got a black cat's bone;
I said black cat's—
I mean bone;
I believe to my soul my man's got a black cat's bone;
Every time I leave I gotta come back home.

Presently, Paul was rejoined by the waiter.

I'm sorry, Mr. Moody, he was apologizing. I hope you'll understand. I don't want to argue with him. He's dangerously strong when he's drunk.

Does he come here often? Paul demanded, dazed.

Every day for two weeks. Never saw him in my life before that. It's easy to tell he ain't used to drink. It hits him hard, makes him very ugly, sir. Sometimes he breaks things. There was a nasty row last week, sir. He almost killed a man.

Has he. . . has he ever been here with *her?*

Your girl, sir?

Paul's smile was sardonic. Yes, he replied, my. . . girl.

He never saw her before, sir. I'll swear to that. He just went over to your table and sat down. I was serving the filet mignon, sir. I was standing right by the table. He looked at her hard and she caved right in. I tried to tell him it was your table, sir, but she yelled out it was none o' my business, and asked the fellow to sit down. He sat down all right. Then he kissed her. He's got a look in his eyes. . .

I know, said Paul. Does he bring girls here often?

Never, sir. He's always alone and he never picked one up here before. He's a strange case, and he's very strong when he's drunk.

They were interrupted by a furious hubbub in the hall.

You'll let us go upstairs, a man's voice was shouting. I've got a warrant.

I'll tell the cockeyed world we'll go upstairs, a woman shrieked.

What is it? Paul demanded. A raid?

It looks like they're after the girl, sir. Trying to get something on her. If it was federal agents they'd come in here first. You're in luck to be out of it, sir.

Paul grinned. The turn affairs had taken was food for amusement. Apparently, Wintergreen was at last losing her chastity without any trouble on his part, and, fortuitously, he was evading some kind of legal wrath. He lighted a cigarette.

Come on, he urged the waiter. I want to see the fun.

He led the way to the corridor. The search party had ascended the stairs and at present were audibly demanding admittance to a closed room. Presently, Paul heard the door crack. The detectives were forcing it with their shoulders.

Backing against the wall Paul went on up until he could see the men at work. A young woman stood by screaming advice couched in coruscating slang. At last, with a shower of splinters and a wooden groan, the door gave way. Gunnar, partially undressed, the huge muscles bulging on his arms, loomed in the opening.

Another step, and by God, I'll kill you all! he threatened.

He can do it, too, the waiter suggested. Better leave him alone.

We got what we come for, one of the detectives announced. We got the evidence.

You've ruined her, Paul Moody, the woman shrieked, and you'll pay the penalty.

I'm not Paul Moody, Gunnar protested stubbornly.

You get to hell out of here, Lottie Coulter! Wintergreen, in her chemise, flaming with wrath, appeared behind her champion in the doorway. How dare you do this to me!

Don't high hat me, Winter. You told me to come yourself! You tipped me off.

I told you to find me and Paul. I said nothing whatever about this gentleman.

You mean. . . ? Lottie gasped, falteringly.

I mean you're a damn fool!

Paul, who in the confusion had escaped attention, slunk down the stairs. Lighting another cigarette, he strolled slowly out of the house.

Whew! he muttered. What an escape!

He rejoined Consuelo and Miss Graves.

You can't see him now, he informed the child. It's impossible. Suppose you let me take you home.

Then I'll lose him again, Consuelo sobbed. I can't bear to lose him again.

I'm afraid we've all lost him, Paul asserted gravely.

What do you mean? Has he killed himself?

Paul reflected. His thoughts rapidly flew back to the evening he had discovered Gunnar in the furnace-room. He recalled, as in a daze, the occasions on which they had met since. And, finally, a vision of what he had just seen in the inn passed before his eyes. It was all too much for his understanding. He mopped his perspiring face with his handkerchief.

I don't know, he replied.

New York
October 16, 1924

A Note About the Author

Carl Van Vechten (1880–1964) was an American photographer, writer, and patron of the Harlem Renaissance. Born in Cedar Rapids, Iowa, Van Vechten was raised in a wealthy, highly educated family. After graduating from high school, he enrolled at the University of Chicago to study art and music, and spent much of his time writing for the college newspaper. In 1903, he took up a position as a columnist for the *Chicago American*, but was fired three years later for his difficult writing style. He moved to New York in 1906 to work as a music critic for *The New York Times*, focusing on opera and taking a leave of absence to travel through Europe the following year. Van Vechten's work as a critic coincided with the careers of some of the twentieth century's greatest artists—the dancer Isadora Duncan; Russian prima ballerina Anna Pavlovna; and Gertrude Stein, a writer and one of Van Vechten's closest friends. Van Vechten, who wrote an influential essay titled "How to Read Gertrude Stein," would become Stein's literary executor following her death in 1946. He is perhaps most notable for his promotion and patronage of some of the Harlem Renaissance's leading artists, including Paul Robeson and Richard Wright. In addition to his photographic portraits of such figures as Langston Hughes, Ella Fitzgerald, Zora Neale Hurston, Marcel Duchamp, and Frida Kahlo, Van Vechten was the author of several novels, including *Peter Whiffle* (1922) and *Firecrackers: A Realistic Novel* (1925).

A Note from the Publisher

Spanning many genres, from non-fiction essays to literature classics to children's books and lyric poetry, Mint Edition books showcase the master works of our time in a modern new package. The text is freshly typeset, is clean and easy to read, and features a new note about the author in each volume. Many books also include exclusive new introductory material. Every book boasts a striking new cover, which makes it as appropriate for collecting as it is for gift giving. Mint Edition books are only printed when a reader orders them, so natural resources are not wasted. We're proud that our books are never manufactured in excess and exist only in the exact quantity they need to be read and enjoyed.

bookfinity™

www.ingramcontent.com/pod-product-compliance
Lightning Source LLC
Chambersburg PA
CBHW030600310726
48979CB00003B/518
9781513132860